THE STONEBRIDGE MYSTERIES

-2-

DEAD IN THE WATER

CHRIS MCDONALD

RED DOG UK

Published by RED DOG PRESS 2021

Copyright © Chris McDonald 2021

Chris McDonald has asserted his right under the Copyright, Designs and Patents Act, 1988 to be identified as the author of this work

This book is sold subject to the condition that it shall not by way of trade or otherwise, be lent, resold, hired out, or otherwise circulated without the publisher's prior consent in any form of binding or cover other than that in which it is published and without a similar condition including this condition being imposed on the subsequent purchaser

First Edition

Paperback ISBN 978-1-914480-42-3

Ebook ISBN 978-1-913331-86-3

www.reddogpress.co.uk

1

COLD IS THE WATER

MATTHEW HENDERSON WAS in a bad mood as he watched the lights from the houses on the other side of the river reflect and distort in the dark water.

Tonight's practice had been a disaster.

With the race so close, he had expected more effort and urgency from the team. As captain, it was his job to get them going, but seemingly no matter what he tried tonight, it wasn't getting through.

He'd started with a rousing team talk at the beginning of the evening, keen to get everyone in the mood. The others had sat on the wooden benches in the club house, nodding their heads, though Matthew could tell the vibe was off—they were simply going through the motions.

He'd shrugged it off, thinking perhaps that they just wanted to get out onto the water. But that hadn't been the case either. Once in the boat, there'd been the same level of lethargy. The strokes were not in time and the cox looked like he'd been on a massive bender the night before, his face green before they'd even pushed off from the bank.

Matthew had cut the practice short and insisted on a team meeting once back on dry land. Upon reaching the jetty, they'd tethered the nine-man rowing boat and the single seater canoe to the moorings and had all stomped back to the building.

He'd started gently—softly, softly, catchy monkey and all that—though, when he realised his words were barely making a ripple let alone the waves he wanted, Matthew had unleashed a storm. He'd given the team a collective bollocking and had then moved on to individual reprimands. By the time he was finished, his face was blotchy and his throat raw.

'Catch yourself on!' one of the team had shouted back.

'It's hardly the bloody Olympics, is it?' another had muttered, before storming out.

One or two followed but the rest had remained and a huge argument had followed. Hurtful words had been exchanged and the night might even have ended in violence, had a few of the lads not got between Simon, the vice-captain of the team, and Matthew.

Once things had calmed slightly, he'd dismissed them all with a warning—come back tomorrow with a better attitude or he'd find more suitable team mates who shared his drive.

And now, as he walked down the jetty towards the small canoe, his headtorch providing the only light, he thought about the accusations that had been levelled at him.

That he cared too much.

That he wasn't a good captain.

That he was only doing this for the prize money, anyway.

Screw them, he thought, pushing the thoughts from his mind as he bent down to pull the canoe from the water.

And then, he heard something.

A noise from near the building.

He let go of the canoe and straightened up, peering in the direction the noise had come from, though the headtorch's beam was no match for the night's inky blanket.

He couldn't see anything.

'Is somebody there?' he called into the black, but he received no reply.

We need to get that security light fixed, he thought, and dismissed the noise as nothing more than an animal scurrying across the gravel. He once again turned his attention to the canoe bobbing in the freezing cold water.

His fingers closed around the rope securing it to the post and as he pulled it towards him, he heard rapid footsteps behind him on the wooden jetty.

He turned from his task once more to be greeted by a familiar face.

'Back for another round, are you?' Matthew said, drawing himself to his full height, hoping to be as intimidating as possible.

'I just thought you might've… I don't know… reconsidered.'

'I thought I was pretty clear earlier when I told you to f…'

His sentence was cut short as the figure lunged at him, though he was too slow to defend himself.

A hefty whack was delivered to the front of his head, and as he struggled to make sense of what was happening, he felt the solid ground disappear from below him. Pain surged up his back as he collided heavily with the edge of the jetty, before tumbling into the river. His senses immediately became overloaded by the shock of how cold the water was.

His head bobbed below the waterline and, as he resurfaced, he fought hard to take in as much air as possible, though already his body was beginning to shut down.

The person on the jetty was on their knees, holding out a hand that Matthew couldn't reach, and yelling something, though the words were lost on the wind.

The river was playing with Matthew now; tossing him around like a ragdoll, away from the safety of the river bank and away from the helping hand.

The same hand that had just sentenced him to his death.

2

FORE!

THE SUN WAS shining and not a cloud was to be found in the sky above the Stonebridge Memorial Golf Club—a sprawling eighteen-hole links course on the north coast of Northern Ireland.

Many of the holes hugged the rugged coastline, though this was not something Harry Gallagher had had to concern himself with. Every shot he had hit during his round so far had travelled as straight as an arrow along the fairway.

His approach on the ninth hole was no different. There sat the little white, dimpled ball; dead centre. He strode along the short grass with a smile on his face and the warmth on his back, quietly plotting his next shot.

He reached his ball and looked up, calculating the distance to the pin. He was no expert, but he held a finger up to check the wind speed and direction. Really, he had no idea what he was doing, but it made him look professional and he knew it would be annoying the life out of his friend.

He pulled a pitching wedge from his bag and took a few practice swings, the air around him making a swooshing sound as his club cut through it. Happy with his movement, he approached the ball and mentally prepared himself, before bringing the club down and making perfect contact.

He watched as the ball sailed in a perfect arc before bouncing off the top of the mound at the front of the green and rolling to a stop a few feet from the flag. He put the club between his legs and paraded around as if he was riding a horse. He knew his friend was watching, so he yeehawed loudly and slapped his bottom for extra comedic effect.

He looked around to see if Gary was enjoying his enthusiastic celebrations and was met with a sullen face.

I suppose I'd be annoyed too if my scorecard looked like his, thought Harry.

He replaced the club in the bag, hoisted it onto his shoulder and carried it across to the long grass to help Gary search for his ball. The vegetation was thick and it took them both a few minutes of poking around to locate it.

'Ha, good luck with that shot,' Harry said.

Gary simply huffed and chose his club. With his mood growing worse by the second, he didn't bother with a practice swing. Instead, he swung wildly, smacking the top of the ball which simply served to drive it deeper into the rough.

'That counts as a shot,' laughed Harry.

'Can't I just move it?' Gary asked. 'I'm never getting it out of here.'

Harry considered this for a moment, holding his thumb out sideways like the emperor in Gladiator, before jerking it skywards.

'Normally I'd say no, but since you've got no chance of catching me, I'll be kind.'

'You're far too generous, Arseholius,' Gary replied.

His current ball was deep in prickly gorse, and it looked like he didn't want to add injury to insult. Those spikes would make mincemeat of his delicate hands.

Instead, he turned his back on that one and reached into the front pocket of his golf bag, his hand closing around another ball. He had almost run out, having lost an unholy amount already today. He chose a flat spot on the fairway and dropped his latest victim. He breathed deeply and took some time to consider which club to use.

'I chose a pitching wedge, but you'll probably need a bit more power,' Harry interrupted, unable to contain himself.

'It'll be your kneecaps getting hit rather than this ball if you don't shut it,' Gary replied, causing Harry to howl with laughter.

Gary approached the ball and swung. It followed a similar path to Harry's, though in an effort to get to the flag he'd put a bit too much into his backswing. Rather than bob onto the green, it had skidded across the slick surface and fallen off the back.

Towards the edge of the cliff.

Gary threw his club on the ground and mumbled obscenities as he marched off towards it. Harry grabbed the bags and followed him, trying not to laugh. He knew better than to make another jibe—his friend seemed close to the edge.

Literally and figuratively.

'Oh my God!' screamed Gary, leaping away from the clifftop.

'Don't worry, man. If you've lost your last ball, I'll lend you one. Has it gone in the sea?' Harry replied, reaching his friend. His brow furrowed as he noticed how pale Gary had become.

Harry carefully approached the edge and peeked over, immediately seeing the source of Gary's surprise.

On the rocks at the bottom of the cliff, where the mouth of the River Bann meets the sea, lay a body. The exposed arms and legs were a mottled grey and the navy vest and shorts were soaked against the skin. One shoe was missing and the face looked to be covered in blood.

From his vantage point, Harry couldn't make out who it was.

One thing was for sure, though. Whoever it was, was no longer in the land of the living.

'Call the police,' Harry managed, before throwing up in a nearby shrub.

3

MADE OF THE WHYTE STUFF

ADAM WHYTE STRODE across the grass pushing the lawnmower. He moved the cord out of his way and continued, smiling to himself as he imagined a football pitch with its intricate patterns.

Mrs Laverty's lawn wasn't *that* big, but large enough to keep him busy for another half an hour or so. He looked at the house and saw the corner of the curtain twitch. The lady of the house may be old, but she had high standards and the reactions of an owl. He laughed to himself before noticing clumps of grass starting to form, so he paused to empty the collected grass into one of his heavy-duty sacks.

Once the lawnmower's basket was reattached, he continued with his job. His thoughts turned to all that had happened in the past month, since he and his friend Colin had solved a murder case. They'd become local celebrities for a few weeks and been in the newspapers, much to the local police's annoyance who'd written the death off as accidental and had been made to look foolish by a couple of amateur sleuths.

In the weeks that had followed the case, his attitude to life had changed. Gone was the young man who was happy to waste his days on the sofa. In his place was the new and improved Adam Whyte. The Adam Whyte who had set up his own garden maintenance business and, for the past two weeks, had gone from house to house, weeding, mowing lawns and brushing the leaves that had begun to fall as Summer made way for Autumn.

Most of his customers were little old ladies who couldn't manage with the more demanding aspects of gardening any longer. He'd do the dirty work while they tended to the flower beds, which suited him down to the ground. He enjoyed their conversations and the chocolatey treats they'd often pass his way.

Mrs Laverty was the only one who made him feel like he was in a Diet Coke advert by spying on him as he went about his work. Still, she paid him well and never insisted on him being topless, which was a bonus for the whole street. No one needed to see what was under his T-shirt.

As he was hoisting the lawnmower into the boot of his car, his phone rang. Cursing, he set the lawnmower back on the driveway and reached into his pocket. He didn't recognise the number.

'Hello,' he answered.

'Hi, is this Adam?'

He confirmed that it was. The voice sounded younger than his usual clientele. There was a pause before she continued.

'This is Elena Henderson. I was wondering if we could meet? There is something I'd like to discuss with you.'

'All my services are on my website,' Adam said. 'Is it grass you want cutting or…'

'No, it's not that,' the voice interrupted. 'I'd like to talk about my husband's death.'

Henderson.

It only dawned on Adam once she'd repeated her surname.

Matthew Henderson was the name of the man whose body had been found by two golfers. Adam's mum had worked with his mum years ago and she'd spoken warmly of Matthew. She'd even babysat him on numerous occasions. The news had caused her to be extra clingy for a week, always checking where Adam was going when he was heading out.

'I was sorry to hear about Matthew,' Adam said. 'But, I'm not sure what help I could be to you.'

'I've read about you. How you helped your friend. I thought you might be able to do the same for me,' she said. 'Can we meet this afternoon? Say, three o'clock?'

Adam thought about his schedule. Mr McCullough would have his head if he didn't cut his grass. Today was the old man's turn to host his book group and the state of the garden was something of vast importance. The others couldn't arrive to find grass longer than two inches! Perish the thought!

'Better make it four o'clock,' Adam said, his interest suitably piqued.

ADAM CHECKED HIS watch and hurried up the main street of Stonebridge towards his favourite café, The Last Drop. He wasn't a massive fan of hot drinks, but the double chocolate muffins were to die for.

He joined the short queue and wondered if picking at a muffin during a conversation about a dead spouse was bad form. He picked up an ice-cold Coke and eyed the cake display, deciding against it.

He paid and made his way to a table by the window which looked out onto the bustling, cobbled streets of his hometown. He watched people scurry past, some clearly with somewhere to be and others happy to drift lazily from shop to shop, waiting for something to catch their eye.

The bell above the door shook him from his thoughts. A tall, attractive woman with dark hair and a red, woollen coat had just entered. She scanned the coffee shop before her eyes settled on Adam. She gave him a quick wave and pointed to the queue.

What am I doing here? Adam thought to himself, suddenly feeling out of his depth.

This poor woman had lost her husband a few short weeks ago and, for some reason, she wanted to meet him based on what she'd read about the Daniel Costello case.

He breathed deeply, trying, and failing, to settle his nerves.

A few minutes later, she sank into the seat opposite him and set her steaming mug of hot chocolate on the table. She looked him up and down and an uncertain expression drifted across her face.

She probably wasn't expecting a scrawny, short-arsed twenty something, he thought.

'Thanks for meeting me,' she said, as she unravelled the scarf from around her neck and set it on the unoccupied chair between them.

'No problem,' Adam replied.

She bit her lower lip, as if uncertain how to begin whatever it was she had to say.

'Okay,' she said, finally. 'Well… as I'm sure you know, my husband, Matthew, was found dead a few weeks ago. His body was washed up on some rocks by the golf course.'

'I read about it,' Adam said. 'I'm really sorry.'

She accepted his sympathies with a small nod of her head.

'I'm sure you also read that the police investigated it and decided it was an accidental drowning. That he simply fell into the river after training and got taken by the current.'

'Training?' Adam repeated.

'Matthew was the captain of the Stonebridge rowing team.'

The Stonebridge Regatta weekend was one of the biggest events in the town's calendar. Each year, Stonebridge took on neighbouring Meadowfield in a rowing race on the River Bann, from the Old Bridge to the Millennium Bridge—a distance of just over two miles.

The Oxford-Cambridge Boat Race paled in comparison to how seriously this race was taken by the respective teams. And how much it meant to the people of the bordering towns.

It was a rivalry for the ages and for many years it was simply for bragging rights, but a few years ago, a local business had upped the ante.

Whichever team won got to share five thousand pounds.

'And you don't agree with the police?' Adam said.

'No. Matthew was always so careful around the water. As captain, he set the example. He never shut up about water safety. I just can't believe that he'd slip and fall into the river, it's just not him.'

'And, so…'

'So, what do I want from you?' she interrupted. 'I was wondering if you would… look into things… ask a few questions.'

'You think he was murdered?'

The last word came out as a whisper.

'I do,' she nodded.

Adam felt uneasy. It wasn't that he didn't want to help her, God knows she was obviously hurting. It's just that, he wasn't qualified. He was a gardener, not a private investigator.

'I can pay you,' she said, reaching into her purse, as if sensing his reluctance.

'No,' he said, waving his hand. 'Look, I'll ask around but I can't promise anything.'

She smiled warmly at him, tears threatening to wet her eyes. In order to appear somewhat capable, Adam asked for some background information on Matthew and his death. Fifteen minutes later, Elena rose from her seat and left the café.

Adam sat for a few minutes, digesting the information he'd been given and cursing himself for agreeing to help. He pushed himself out of his seat and walked to the counter, where he ordered two muffins.

When he had finished stuffing his face, he walked out into the dying daylight and pulled out his phone. If he was investigating, he'd need his trusty partner. He found his best friend's number and pressed call, knowing that he'd be keen for another adventure.

4

ELENA HENDERSON'S THEORY EXPLORED

'ABSOLUTELY NOT,' said Colin.

He listened to Adam witter away on the other end of the phone, barely pausing for breath. When Colin tried to interject, Adam simply spoke over him. When he could take no more, he pressed the red button and cut the call. He stuffed the phone back into his locker and left the staff room, annoyed that the phone call had taken up most of his short break.

He walked down the steps and made his way into the lounge of the Stonebridge Retirement Home, his place of work. He'd been here for a number of years and loved the place—or more correctly, the people. Their bodies may be failing, but their minds weren't. They were still razor sharp and desperately funny and Colin loved each and every one of them.

Most of the residents were sitting in their seats, watching an episode of The Antiques Roadshow.

'What are you saying, Mary?' asked Fred.

Mary studied the object currently being scrutinised by the expert on TV—a willow patterned jug.

'Hundred quid,' she guessed.

'Mary says a hundred,' Fred announced, writing her guess down on a pad of paper. 'Any other takers?'

The room erupted into a cacophony of noise, each eager to get their figure heard before the expert cast his judgement, while Fred tried his hardest to note down everyone's estimates. After a minute, he hushed the room in anticipation of the specialist's ruling.

'Thirty-six pounds.' Fred laughed. 'Barry, you were bang on!'

Barry shrugged nonchalantly, though a small smile spread across his face.

'What Barry isn't telling you is that this episode is a repeat of the one him and me watched last week,' Colin said. 'He's seen it before.'

'You prick!' Fred shouted at Barry, who laughed riotously as he raised his middle finger at the group.

The noise died down as Fiona Bruce appeared on screen to introduce the next item. Barry pushed himself out of his seat and followed Colin into a smaller room which was primarily used for craft sessions.

'Rebus, I can't believe you just sold me out,' he laughed.

Since finding out about the role Colin had played in solving Danny Costello's murder a few weeks ago, Barry had stopped calling him by his real name and instead addressed him with a different detective's name whenever the two spoke.

Colin supposed he was doing it to show off how well read he was, and he secretly liked it.

'I can't believe you were trying to deceive those nice ladies in there,' Colin winked.

Barry sat down on one of the wingback chairs and watched Colin clear the table.

'You seem preoccupied, Foley,' Barry said.

'Foley?' Colin replied. 'I've not heard that one before.'

'My daughter has got me into these audiobooks. It means I can lie in my bed like a lazy bugger and have some celebrity read the story to me. This latest one is a cracker. I can't remember the name of it, though. Something about trees by a fella called Bob Barker.'

'Isn't he the American game show host?'

'I might be getting the names mixed up,' Barry shrugged. 'Anyway, don't change the subject. What's eating you?'

'I've just had a phone call from Adam. He's trying to talk me into helping him out with something.'

'Something interesting?'

'Potentially. Do you remember that body they found a few weeks ago in the river?'

Barry nodded. Colin considered how much information to relinquish. He knew that Barry didn't have a hold of his tongue and whatever he told him would be passed around the other residents like wildfire.

'Well, apparently his wife called Adam today and told him that she thinks the death was suspicious, even though the police don't. She's asked him to look into it and he's asked me to help.'

'And you're not going to?'

Barry seemed surprised.

'Why would I?'

'Son, I hope you don't mind me saying, but you spend your days with a load of old farts who have one foot in the grave and another on a banana skin. If I'm right, you don't have a lassie either, so where is the excitement in your life?'

Colin shrugged.

'Exactly. You want my advice? Go and help your friend. It might come to nothing, but at least it'll get you off the GameBoy.'

'Alright. I'll call him back and tell him I'm in. If anyone asks, I've gone to the toilet, alright?'

Barry winked at him as he left the room.

THIS WAS THE first time Colin had been in The Otter since it had been refurbished. They'd done a decent job—the character of the place remained; the brickwork and the fireplaces endured but your feet didn't stick to the carpet anymore. It was win-win.

Adam was sitting at their usual table in the corner of the room, as was a fizzing pint of lager. Colin plonked himself down in the chair and took a swift sup.

'So,' he said, replacing his glass on the table. 'What have we got?'

Adam explained what had happened, starting with the phone call from Elena and ending with the muffins.

'Two?' Colin said, more preoccupied with his friend's greed than the dead man.

'I was stressed and I couldn't decide which flavour to get, so I got both. Don't judge me.'

'So, what's next?'

'Well, after I met with Elena, I rang Daz.'

Darren Ringley was their friend and member of the Police Service of Northern Ireland.

'And what did Daz have to say?'

'I asked him about the circumstances around the discovery of the body—when he was found, when they thought he had died, all that stuff. Elena reported him missing on the 17th September and his body was found on the 19th. The injuries were consistent with those usually suffered after a fall—bruising on the arse and legs and a broken coccyx. He also had a gash on his head from where he bashed it on a rock on his way into the water. They think it probably knocked him out—that's why they reckon he drowned. Apparently, he was a pretty good swimmer and would've stood a good chance of getting out, even with the currents.'

'It sounds accidental to me,' Colin said, having weighed up the information.

'It sounds it, but when you think of the timing, it's hard to know. The boat race is only a few weeks away…'

'You can't think that someone would've killed Matthew just to win a race though?'

'Stranger things have happened,' Adam said.

'In ganglands, maybe, but not in Stonebridge.'

'Look, it could be nothing, but Elena seemed pretty sure that foul play was involved. She kept going on about how safety conscious he was and stuff.'

Colin took another pull from his pint.

'Okay, I suppose it can't hurt to look into it. Where do we start?'

'That's the spirit,' Adam said, clapping him on the back. 'I've got a few ideas, but I think we need to see where he fell in. Elena said he was always the last one at the rowing sheds, making sure the equipment was all locked away safely and what have you. I say we pay a little visit there—that'll help us decide if the investigation has legs.'

With no other information currently available, talk turned to football and one pint became two, and two became too many. At last orders, they arranged a time to meet at the sheds, had one more pint and then made their unsteady way home.

5

DOWN TO THE RIVER

ADAM GROANED AS the sound of his ringtone clattered around his head. He rolled over, grabbed the phone off his bedside table and answered it without checking who it was.

'Still on for this morning?' Colin asked.

'Yep,' Adam croaked, stifling a yawn and hearing the thickness in his voice. 'I'm just about to get in the car.'

Colin laughed.

'You're such a bad liar. You're still in your pit, aren't you? Do you want to push it back an hour?'

Adam agreed that that course of action would probably be for the best before hanging up and falling back onto his pillow. His eyes were beginning to close when his phone rang again. He put it to his ear.

'Get up, now,' Colin said, and hung up.

IT WAS A crisp Autumn day and Colin was sitting on a bench that overlooked the grey, fast flowing river. He pulled the hood of his coat up against the wind and finished checking a few things on his phone as a car pulled into the rowing club's car park.

He watched as Adam pulled his rusty Clio into a space and dragged himself out of it, before traipsing over to the bench. He pointed at the other car in the car park, a sporty Fiesta, and Colin shrugged.

'I'm going teetotal,' Adam said as he plonked himself onto the seat and massaging his temples.

'We only had five pints.'

Instead of answering, Adam took in a deep, mollifying breath of fresh air.

'So,' Colin said, 'what is it that we're looking for?'

'We need to decide whether or not it's possible that Matthew could have simply fallen in. I just want a look around to see how steep the bank is, how close the building is to the water, that kind of thing.'

With that, they pushed themselves from the bench and walked towards the rowing centre.

It was a two-storey building. The bottom half was made from red brick and had three huge, metallic shuttered doors along its front, facing onto the bank of the river. Presumably this is where the rowing boats were stored. The top half was smoothly rendered and painted white, though some time ago. Large windows overlooked the body of water and a balcony jutted out, housing a number of tables and chairs.

Colin tried the front door but it was locked, as were all the others.

Good, he thought, *less chance of being disturbed.*

They circled the building and met at the side facing the water. The bank wasn't steep and the water was far enough away from the building that a trip would've resulted in a fall onto concrete, rather than into water.

'I checked the weather on the date Elena told you,' Colin said. 'On the 17th September, it was sunny, as were the days leading up to it. Even if he was mucking about down near the water, the grass would've been dry, so the chances of slipping would've been minimal.'

Adam nodded and Colin followed him out onto the wooden jetty which sat above the river. They watched their broken reflections in the water for a while before Adam spoke.

'There are no cameras on the building, so we have no hope of any CCTV.'

'So, what are you thinking?'

Adam puffed out his cheeks.

'It's hard to know. It seems unlikely that a safety freak could've accidentally fallen in, given how far away the building is. The water doesn't get deep for a while either, so if he'd slipped in, the water would've been shallow enough for him to simply get up from.'

'Unless he was dead before he was dropped in?'

'No,' Adam said, shaking his head. 'Daz said that the official cause of death was drowning. His lungs were full of water. So, if someone else was involved, they dumped him in the river while he was still alive.'

'That might account for the bruises. Maybe he had a fight with someone on the bank and was knocked out. Maybe whoever it was thought they'd killed him and panicked, so threw him in the water and let the river carry him away.'

'Or, it could just be a horrible accident.'

Disappointed that the answer wasn't being made clearer by the environment, they left the jetty and returned to the car park.

A tall, dark haired man with glasses slipping down the bridge of his nose was standing by the Fiesta, key in hand. He looked around when he heard Colin and Adam approach and gave them a friendly wave.

'How are you, lads?'

'Alright, thanks,' Colin answered. 'Yourself?'

'Been better. I had a few too many last night at the social club,' he pointed at the top half of the building. 'I reckon I'm just about safe to drive now.'

'Are you part of the rowing team?'

The man nodded.

'Theo Jamieson,' he said, extending a hand which they both shook while introducing themselves.

'Theo,' said Colin. 'Do you mind if we ask you a few questions?'

THOUGH HE DIDN'T like the taste of it, the smell of brewing coffee behind the counter of the café was making Adam feel almost human again and he nearly pounced on the waiter when he delivered his hot chocolate.

He took a small sip and felt the sugar take hold immediately.

Theo sat opposite them making it feel and look like a job interview.

Perhaps not the best way to put him at ease, thought Adam.

'Thanks for agreeing to chat to us,' Adam said with a smile. 'We just have a few questions about Matthew.'

Theo's face fell.

'What about him? Are you the police?'

'We're not with the police, no, but we are looking into what happened to him.'

'Didn't the police say that it was accidental drowning?'

'They did,' Colin said. 'But we may have a different opinion.'

'Well, fire away,' Theo answered.

'How did you know Matthew?'

'Through the club. I only joined last year so this would've been my first race. I was proper looking forward to it, but it looks like it's going to be cancelled.'

'Did you socialise?'

'Not really. We'd sometimes have a few pints after training, but the sessions were so intense, I'd usually prefer to go home and have a hot bath. Made it easier on the muscles the next day. Sometimes, as captain, he'd make us stay for a drink. For team bonding and whatnot.'

'And what was Matthew like?'

Theo's eyes fell to the table and he began to chew his bottom lip.

'Umm… he was, alright.'

'But not really?' Colin prodded.

'Well, I don't want to speak ill of the dead, but it seemed like being captain gave him some sort of ego trip. He wasn't well liked because he spoke down to people. As the new boy, I took it with a pinch of salt, got my head down and worked hard, but others weren't so forgiving.'

'How do you mean?'

'He handled situations badly. Anytime he felt like someone was trying to undermine him, or if he thought someone wasn't pulling their weight, he went off on one. That kind of thing wears you down over time. There have been a couple of drunken fights—nothing bad—but a few punches have been thrown in the heat of the moment.'

'Anyone in particular?'

'Most have had a run in with him at some stage, but recently it's been mainly Craig and Simon who've taken the brunt of it.'

'Do you think either of them would've…' Adam lowered his voice. '…killed him?'

'Bloody hell,' said Theo, his cheeks reddening. 'No, people don't get murdered in Stonebridge. Look, he was always the one there at the end of the practice sessions. He was the one who put the boats away and made sure everything was locked up. He probably slipped on the jetty, that's all there is to it.'

Theo lifted his coffee cup and drank the remainder in one gulp.

'I wouldn't waste any more of your time looking into it,' he said, before bidding Colin and Adam farewell and making his way to the door. They watched him walk past the window and disappear.

'Bit of an abrupt ending,' Colin said.

'Yeah, it seemed like he realised he'd said too much.'

They sat for a few silent minutes, lost in their own thoughts. In Adam's mind, Matthew's death was not the cut and dry accident that it appeared to be. Resentful team mates and fist fights were not commonplace in any team he'd been part of and definitely hinted that something wasn't right here.

'What next?' Colin asked.

'We find Craig and Simon and hope that they talk to us.'

6

LEGWORK

AN EPISODE OF Sherlock Adam had seen a million times was playing in the background as he leafed through the Stonebridge Regatta commemorative programme from 2019.

The glossy magazine belonged to his mum's collection. She hadn't missed one in twenty-four years and was excited to collect her twenty-fifth in a few weeks' time.

If it went ahead, of course.

He flipped to the middle pages where the teams for that year's race were displayed. Photographs of each member stared out at him. Some smiling with a twinkle in their eye. Others with a slight scowl on their face, as if trying to intimidate the opposition.

Adam surveyed the Stonebridge team.

Matthew Henderson was in the middle, holding the gleaming cup they'd won the previous year, with a huge grin plastered across his face. Intense, dark eyes peered out from under a heavy brow.

Beside the picture, some information was listed. Things like how many years he'd been part of the team and what his proudest moment was. Alongside it was some trivia. Bland stuff, really. What his favourite restaurant was (The Ramore) and what he'd do with one million pounds (buy a Ferrari and move to LA).

Adam moved his attention to the other rowers.

Among them, were Craig and Simon.

Adam studied their smirking faces and turned his attention to the trivia section, hoping something would leap out that could give him an *in*.

Which, for Craig, it did.

He pulled out his phone and dialled Colin's number.

'Meet me at Lucky's tonight,' he said when the phone had been answered.

'Why?'

'Because I've got a plan.'

LUCKY'S WAS THE sports bar in the centre of Stonebridge. The owners had a huge love for all things American and had decked out the interior of the bar with anything starred or striped.

The walls were decorated with licence plates from all fifty states as well as promotional drink signs featuring American sporting royalty. Guest lagers from the US, with their exotic flavours and their colourful pump clips, filled the beer pumps frequently.

Amongst all of this were a number of huge plasma televisions, showing sport constantly. Tonight, a pivotal Premier League match between table topping Liverpool and second placed Manchester City was being shown.

Which was handy, because Craig not only worked at the bar, but also supported Liverpool.

As did Adam.

COLIN AND ADAM met outside the bar. Colin raised an eyebrow at what his friend was wearing—the newest kit the Reds had put out.

'How much did that set you back?' Colin asked.

'Seventy quid.'

'Jesus. I thought you were broke?'

'Well, Mrs Jones gave me a wee bonus for trimming her bush for her, so I thought I'd treat myself. And, you've not even seen the best bit yet.'

Adam shrugged off his coat and turned around to show Colin the pièce de résistance. The gale of laughter was not the reaction he'd expected.

'Who gets the names of players on the back of their shirts anymore? What are you? Seven years old?'

'He was our top scorer last year.'

'Did you have to pay extra for that?'

Adam replied quietly.

'What was that?' Colin said, cupping his ear.

'I said it was an extra fifteen quid.'

'Good God, you are a sad act. Put your coat on so no one sees what you've done or I'm not going in with you.'

Colin waited until Adam had done as he was asked before pushing the door open.

THEY MADE THEIR way through the crowd and squeezed into a booth that not only offered them a good view of a television, but also of the bar.

Craig was there behind it, pouring a pint and talking animatedly to the waiting customer. His dark hair, widows peak and pale complexion combined to make him look like Dracula.

Adam tore his eyes away from the barman and looked through the American themed menu.

'I think I might have a milkshake,' Adam said.

'You're here to question a possible murder suspect,' replied Colin. 'If you go up to him wearing your ridiculous football top with your favourite player on the back and order a milkshake instead of a beer, he might mistake you for a child and turf you out.'

'But my head is still sore from last night.'

Colin fixed him with a glare that left the matter resolved.

Beer it was.

Adam shuffled along the squeaky leather seat and left the booth. He walked to the bar and stood with one arm atop it, his eyes on the television mounted above the spirits. The pundit's lively voice boomed through the speakers, announcing which players had made the team sheet.

'Can I get you anything, mate?'

Adam lowered his gaze to meet Craig's.

'Two pints of Harp, please.'

As Craig poured the first pint, Adam unzipped his jacket slightly. He noticed the barman's eyes drift to his new t-shirt.

'Nice top, man,' Craig said. 'I like the bit of green on it.'

'Yeah, Nike have done a good job. Better than last year's kit, anyway.'

Craig flipped the handle of the pump and handed the full pint glass across the bar. He placed the empty below the pump and pushed the handle again.

'What do you think of our chances tonight?' Adam asked.

'I've got a fiver on us to win 2-1, so I've got my fingers crossed.'

Adam saw an in.

'Ah, betting man. What do you reckon about this year's rowing race then? Who do you fancy?'

Craig puffed out his chest proudly.

'I'm actually on the Stonebridge team, so I couldn't bet if I wanted to. Smart man's money is on the other team.'

'Why?' Adam asked, playing ignorant.

Craig looked at him like he'd sprouted a second head.

'Have you been living under a rock? Our captain fell in the river and drowned. We've had to appoint a temporary captain while we find a full-time replacement. It's been chaos.'

'Sorry to hear,' Adam said, taking a sip from his pint. 'Now that you mention it, the story is coming back to me. I've heard a few rumours that Michael…'

'Matthew.'

'Matthew, that's it. I've heard rumours that say he might not have fallen in. That he was maybe… pushed.'

'Bollocks,' said Craig.

'You don't think anyone would want to hurt him?'

'There's a difference between hurting and killing. I imagine quite a few of the team wouldn't have minded a free swing at him.'

'Why?'

'He was hard on us. He wanted to win, no matter the cost. He didn't care about friendships. As a matter of fact, him and me were best friends until he became captain.'

'Why would that stop you being friends?'

'He became paranoid that I wanted to take the title from him. Strange, really. He stopped talking to me and moved my position in the boat so that I was far away from him.'

Craig peeled away to pour a drink for another customer before returning. Adam wasn't sure why he was being so open with him. Maybe it was cathartic to talk about his friend, or ex-friend's, death.

'You see,' he continued. 'The captain gets the biggest share of the prize money. That's why he was so eager to hold onto the role.'

'Why wouldn't the money be split equally?'

'The captain does a load more work than anyone else. All the admin, the training plans and the organising. The first year the prize money was introduced, that's what the team decided and it stuck.'

Could someone have pushed Matthew to his death for a bit more money?

'Who became captain after Matthew's death?' Adam asked.

'A guy called Simon. One of the long-serving members.'

At that, a large group of raucous lads burst in through the door and made a beeline for the bar. Adam wished Craig luck with his bet before walking back to the booth.

'I thought you were brewing the beer yourself you took so long,' Colin said as he took his pint. 'I take it he told you some stuff?'

Adam spent a few minutes relaying the information he'd just received to his friend.

'So,' Colin said. 'Simon might benefit financially from Matthew's death?

Adam nodded.

'Sounds like we might need to have a chat with him.'

7

THE SHIP HAS AN ANCHOR AND THE CAPTAIN IS A …

MOST OF THE residents had retired to their rooms with a bellyful of food, ready for a mid-afternoon nap while a few had hung around in the main room with their eyes glued to the television.

Colin was using the downtime to crack on with some paperwork. He loved his job and he loved the people, but the incessant filling in of forms was a definite downside. Though, of course, he knew why he had to do it. He'd watched the horrible exposés where someone had gone undercover at a care home and filmed the abuse doled out by bullies who had somehow got a job there.

It made him sick to his stomach.

A knock on the door jerked him back to reality and he smiled at Barry as he made his way into the room and lowered himself slowly into a chair on the other side of the desk.

'How are you, mucker?' Colin asked.

'Not too bad, Poirot. I was just wondering if you've got a case on your hands or not.'

'We just might. Still trying to work out whether or not someone pushed him into the river. We've met a few shady characters and we've been pointed in the direction of another one.'

Barry sat up a bit in his seat, the excitement getting to him.

'Are you going to question him?'

'I'm going to go and have a word.'

Colin had been thinking about how best to approach Simon Holland and had finally settled on a course of action. He told

Barry of his plans and watched a little smile form under the old man's moustache as he nodded his approval.

'I didn't realise you were such a devious fella,' he laughed. 'I'll have to keep an eye on you from now on. I can half-imagine you swiping my daily pills and flogging them to needy lads on street corners.'

COLIN PULLED INTO a space in the car park and got out, aware that the town's shops would soon be locking their doors for the day. He hurried through the narrow alleyway and emerged in the centre of Stonebridge, making his way quickly towards the far end of town.

Holland & Morrow Estate Agents held a small office which was sandwiched between a newsagent that had been in the town forever and a café that seemed to change ownership weekly.

Being a small university town, Stonebridge had a lot of student housing, which was Holland & Morrow's speciality. They also had a stronghold on lodgings for the single professional.

Which was the angle Colin was hoping to use.

While pretending to look at the pictures of houses in the window, he snuck a few glances inside. Simon Holland was sitting at a desk at the back, a phone clamped between his shoulder and ear. His mouth was moving at a mile a minute, no doubt chewing someone's ear off in order to secure a sale.

Colin pushed the door open and walked in.

Simon looked up from his computer screen and flashed a toothy smile at him. He pointed first to the phone and then his watch, before rolling his eyes. He then turned his attention back to his computer screen.

Immediately, Colin formed a dislike for the man. The perfectly tailored suit jacket, the overwhelming stench of aftershave and his Wall Street attitude were all so overblown considering he was running a boutique estate agency in a small town.

While Simon finished his phone call, Colin spent the time looking around the office. It was as if the two owners had decided to divvy up the walls and decorate them how they saw fit. Mr Morrow's half was basic. A few framed certificates were nailed to the wall and a calendar showing the Giant's Causeway hung just behind his tidy desk.

Simon's half on the other hand was like a shrine to himself. Newspaper cuttings about the company fought for space among the many pictures of himself in rowing gear. He was clearly very proud of the Stonebridge team's achievements over the past few years.

'How can I help you, young man?' he asked, as he replaced the receiver.

'I'm looking to move out of my parent's house. I need a bit of space, you know?'

'Ah, I do indeed remember how that felt and how great it was to get a foot on the ladder. You've come to the right place.'

He wheeled himself over to the computer and began typing furiously on the keyboard. His jacket sleeves rode up slightly, revealing gold cufflinks. An S in one cuff and an H in the other.

'Just going to take a few details and then we can begin a bespoke search for your prospective new property.'

Bespoke? thought Colin. *Jesus.*

He answered a series of questions and gave his house search criteria. Truth be told, he had been thinking of moving out for a while. He'd managed to save a healthy amount from his job, and his dad had often said he'd help top up the deposit if needed, so he gave an honest list of things that he would like—may as well kill two birds with one stone.

'Ok,' Simon said. 'Let's see what we've got.'

As he waited for the computer to work its magic, Colin seized his chance. He nodded to the pictures.

'You keen on rowing, then?'

'You could say that. This year will be my tenth with the Stonebridge team—providing it still goes ahead.'

'Are you confident of the win?'

'We were. Before what happened to Matthew.'

Colin nodded sympathetically.

'I imagine what happened must have cast a shadow on everything.'

Simon shrugged, his eyes scanning the monitor, his tongue protruding slightly between his teeth.

'Yeah. He'd been captain for the last few years. It won't be the same without him, but we're determined to win it in his honour.'

'A lot of responsibility on the new captain, I'd imagine.'

'I'm the new captain and I eat responsibility for breakfast.'

Colin let that statement settle, hoping Simon could hear how stupid it sounded.

'There was chat from someone I know that there had been some pretty big bust-ups lately.'

Simon stared resolutely at the computer, though it was clear that he wasn't focussed on the details on the screen. His cheeks had turned rather red, despite the cool temperature.

'Who told you that? Theo?'

Colin remained silent.

'I take that as a yes,' Simon continued. 'Everyone had clashes with everyone, especially on the run up to the actual race. If you didn't think the person beside you or in front of you was putting an honest shift in, you'd tell them. And they'd tell you. That's normal. You want to win so you demand the best from everyone around you.'

'Did Matthew get at you?'

'Course he did. And I got at him. We had a massive barney the night of his death. Like I said, it was normal. We argued and then we made up. It's Theo's first year and I'd honestly be surprised if he comes back. The lad's too wet for this game.'

Colin was aware that this was beginning to sound like a police interrogation so changed his tone. More agony aunt than Gestapo.

'That must be horrible—you having an argument and then him dying.'

'I've made my peace with it. He knew and I knew that it was solely for the good of the team. What happened was… unfortunate.'

Colin nodded.

'Like I said, we're going to win in his honour,' Simon said. 'Despite the antics of those knobs from Meadowfield.'

'What do you mean?'

'They are a bunch of hick farmers who have been trying for months to disrupt our training…' He suddenly looked alarmed. 'Oh, God, you're not from there, are you?'

Colin shook his head.

'Thank God. Well, they call them pranks, and at first, they were small funny things, but at times they've overstepped the mark. Matthew was convinced they were going to end up hurting one of us.'

As Colin was about to press him on what kinds of things the other team had been doing, Simon's computer emitted a small ping. He turned the monitor around so that Colin could see the various properties that fitted his price range and conditions.

They scrolled through a number of pages and Colin picked three that he liked. He checked his shifts at work and booked in viewings with Simon. If the houses came to nothing, it at least gave him more time to question the estate agent.

He left the office feeling as if he'd taken another step in the direction of adulthood.

8

THE WOOD EMPORIUM

ADAM SET DOWN the hedge trimmers and stretched. All the overhead work meant looking up, which meant he'd end up with a sore neck if he wasn't careful. He walked the length the holly bush, cursing when he realised how much more he had to do.

'What was that, dear?' said Mrs Stanley, who must've snuck into the garden on the other side of the holly without Adam noticing.

'Uh… I said I thought I heard a duck.'

'Not round these parts, pet. Maybe a goose flying overhead.'

'Maybe,' Adam said, snatching up the shears again. He replaced his earphones and pressed play on his phone, the harsh metal music immediately attacking his eardrums.

He closed Spotify and noticed a WhatsApp message from his mum which she had sent over two hours ago, according to the time stamp.

Phone me.

Adam's heart began to race. His mum rarely sent messages and when she did, they were lengthy compositions that took an age to trawl through.

Something must be wrong.

He pulled the earphones out of his ears again and phoned his mum straight away. She answered after a few rings.

'Mum, what's wrong?'

'Nothing, dear. Why?'

'Because your short message sounded like something someone might send if they'd managed to escape their kidnapper and didn't have very much time.'

'But, I just wanted you to phone me when you had a minute. What else was I supposed to say?'

'I dunno. Something like "I hope you're having a nice day. When you get a minute, would you mind phoning me. It's nothing important, and I'm definitely not in any mortal danger."'

'What a waste of time.'

'What is?'

'This conversation. All I wanted to do was ask you if you fancied meeting up for lunch today?'

Adam checked the time.

'I'll probably be done here in the next couple of hours, so I could meet you at around one?'

'Perfect,' his mum said, before the line went dead.

Who did she think she was hanging up like that, Jack Bauer? Adam thought as he stuffed the phone back into his pocket and carried on with his work.

THE SQUARE WAS his mum's café of choice—had been since he was a little boy. They'd come every Saturday, sit by the first-floor window and watch the world go by below them.

When he'd entered his teens, the café visits had become less regular. In fact, he couldn't remember the last time the two of them had been here. He smiled across the table at the woman who had raised him single-handedly, on account of his dad leaving one day and never coming back.

He resolved to make more time for her.

The waiter came and set a jacket potato smothered with cheese in front of his mum and a mouth-watering pulled pork panini on Adam's placemat.

Adam wolfed down his food, only realising as he picked up the meat-filled bread just how hungry he had been. His mum took a little longer and when she set down her cutlery, she cleared her throat.

'Adam, I just want to say how proud I am of you for giving something a go. The gardening thing really seems to be taking off and I think it's great that you are showing so much passion for it.'

'Thanks, mum,' he managed through a particularly full mouth. 'Means a lot.'

'I've been reading a hygge book…'

'A what?' Adam interrupted. He didn't know the word she had just said, but it sounded like she was choking on phlegm.

'Hygge. It's a Danish thing, all about recognising how good life is. Anyway, it's got a bit about sleep and de-cluttering and how having lots of electrical things in your bedroom is bad for sleep patterns.'

'Sounds like someone has too much time on their hands.'

'Thank you, Sigmund Freud. I was just telling you this because I thought you might like to turn the third bedroom into an office, you know, to do your invoicing and what have you. You could put your tele and games things in there too and really sort out your bedroom.'

Adam quite liked the thought of sitting at a desk, figuring out how much people owed him. He could sit with his chair tipped back and his feet on the desk, sipping a beer like they did in Mad Men.

'Sounds good. Nice idea, mum.'

'I thought we could go over to The Wood Emporium and have a gander. I bet he's got some nice desks and he's got a sale on at the minute.'

'When does that man *not* have a sale on. He's like a local DFS.'

'Is that a yes?' she asked, rising from her seat.

'It is indeed,' he replied, pulling out the bank card from his pocket. 'Here, let me get this.'

PERCY WOOD WAS the man you came to see if you wanted furniture. His shop was a landmark in Stonebridge—one of the longest serving family businesses left. Only old man Tucker's car garage topped it in terms of longevity, and he was without son. The Tucker name would soon pass, and Wood would take the title.

A little bell above the door tinkled as they entered. The shop was narrow, but long, and housed a wide assortment of furniture. From kitchen tables to oak sideboards, pine wardrobes to sets of drawers, Percy always had whatever you were looking for.

As they made their way past the counter, Adam was relieved to see that the patriarch of the store was not behind it. In his place was his son, Jacob Wood.

Adam could never pin down exactly why he had such an aversion to Percy. If he thought about it, part of it was because he reminded him of Ollivander from the Harry Potter books.

Percy had the same frazzled grey hair and dapper dress sense. He also always seemed to be lurking in the shadows, ready to appear from nowhere so that he could lead you to your chosen piece of furniture.

Jacob was much more lackadaisical, as evidenced by him barely glancing up from his book as Adam and his mum walked past.

'If you need any help, just give me a shout,' Jacob muttered, while turning a page of some pretentious looking tome.

They made their way to the desks and Adam pushed one of the wheely chairs over, taking his place behind a number of tables and pretending to type.

He'd always fancied one of those lights with a brass body and a green glass shade, and so chose the desk he thought it would look best sitting on. It was made of mahogany and he thought the dark wood would really make the light stand out.

'You're sure?' his mum asked, checking for a price tag.

He sized it up one more time, looked quickly at the others and nodded. This beast was the one for him.

They made their way to the counter.

'How can I help you?' asked Jacob, folding the corner of the page he had reached before setting the book down.

'We'd like to buy a desk,' Adam said. 'It's the mahogany one at the back.'

'The one with three drawers?'

Adam confirmed that that was indeed the one he had set his heart on.

While he was sorting the payment and insurance forms, Adam's mum tried to engage Jacob in conversation.

'How is your dad doing?'

'Ah, he's grand. He loves this time of year, what with the boat race and the fête and whatnot so he's taken a bit of time off.'

'Is he presenting the trophy again this year?'

Jacob nodded.

'He is. I think that's the only reason he offered to sponsor the race. Five thousand pounds just to hand over a cup. People must think he's mad.'

'I think it's a good business move,' said Adam. 'Surely most of Stonebridge associate this place with the race weekend.'

'They do, but it doesn't mean they all shop here. A certain Scandinavian outlet in the capital has seen to that. They may be cheaper but they don't have our quality. It's why we constantly seem to have a sale on—we have to do something to compete.'

Silence filled the musty shop.

'Sorry,' Jacob said, rubbing his greying temples. 'I'm ranting. It's just stressful trying to run the business in the age of smartphones and click and collects. Dad expects us to be as prolific as ever, but sadly, brand loyalty is not a thing anymore.'

'Well, you'll always be my first choice for furniture,' Adam's mum said.

Jacob's features rearranged themselves into something resembling a smile, as if the muscles hadn't been forced into this particular formation in quite a long time.

'I appreciate it. Thank you, you've brightened my day.'

And it seemed, they had. For after that, he led them to the back of the shop where a variety of office chairs sat, and offered them a good deal on whichever one Adam fancied.

With delivery arranged and payment made, they left the shop.

'Maybe he'd appreciate a lesson in hygge,' Adam said.

His mum slapped him on the arm.

'Don't be sarcastic with me,' she replied. 'And it's you who is going to need a lesson soon, because it's your job to clear out the back room ready for your new desk.'

9

TÊTE-À-TÊTE

COLIN PUSHED OPEN Adam's bedroom door and was met with an unusual sight. The mounds of dirty clothes that were a mainstay on the floor were gone. As was the widescreen television and the PlayStation. And the beer fridge…

Something wasn't right here.

He heard his name being called from the landing and left the room to find Adam peeking at him from the behind the door in the back bedroom. He walked across the hallway and entered the bedroom, amazed at the transformation.

On nights when the two of them would have a sleepover, drinking beer and playing Football Manager late into the night, this was Colin's bedroom. Usually, a single bed was pushed against one wall and a set of drawers sat against the wall opposite.

Today, it was totally different. Both bits of furniture were gone.

In their place was a sturdy desk made of dark wood, upon which sat Adam's laptop and some files. The flatscreen tv was mounted to the wall above it and a comfortable sofa bed filled most of the rest of the space.

Adam sat in a high-backed leather office chair.

'Nice place you got here,' Colin said, sinking into the sofa.

'Mum is on some hygge thing. She suggested decluttering my room for a better sleeping experience.'

'My dad was talking about that the other day. Is someone trying to brainwash us?'

'Not sure, but I spent yesterday breaking up the bed and getting everything tidy in here. Jacob Wood delivered the desk this morning. Kept going on about customer service. I think he was expecting a tip.'

'Well, I think it looks great in here. Well done, man.'

'Thanks,' said Adam. 'How did it go with Simon?'

'He's an idiot. Bloody loves himself. He's got pictures of himself all over the office walls and possibly worse than that—gold cufflinks with his initials on.'

'That is dreadful,' Adam agreed.

'He told me that him and Matthew had a massive argument the night he died and he didn't seem particularly cut up about the fact they ended their friendship on a sour note. He also said that the Meadowfield team were doing things to try and interfere with their training. Apparently, Matthew was convinced they were going to go too far and end up hurting one of them.'

Adam mulled over the new information silently.

'So, you think his death might've been a prank gone wrong?'

Colin shrugged.

'Who knew rowing could be so rowdy?' Adam laughed. 'Fist fights, arguments, inter-town warfare… next year the regatta will have ultras with flares standing by the riverbank.'

'Aye, and pouring offal from the bridges into the boats. What do we do next?'

'We think, the only way we know how.'

Adam turned the PlayStation on and started a football game. He handed Colin a controller and the two picked their teams. They knocked a few ideas back and forth, each finding a hole in the other's scheme.

Suddenly, Adam gasped and paused the game.

'Oi,' Colin shouted. 'I was just about to score.'

'Never mind about that. I have an idea. One of us could infiltrate the Meadowfield team—go undercover. If we can do that, we'll know whether or not they had a hand in Matthew's death.'

'And when you say "one of us", I'm guessing you actually mean me.'

'Well, if we want to get in with them, it needs to be believable. They'd laugh me out of town, what with my weedy arms and little boy body. But, strapping young lad like you, they'd have you in an instant.'

Colin couldn't argue with the logic.

'What if they find out I'm from Stonebridge?'

'You just badmouth the town—that'll instantly get you brownie points and a one-way ticket onto their boat.'

Colin sighed.

'Okay,' he said, finally. 'I'll find out when their practice times are and head down, try to get in with them.'

'Good man,' said Adam, unpausing the game whilst Colin wasn't quite ready. His defender tackled Colin's striker and booted the ball to safety. Adam received a thump on the arm for his troubles.

'Worth it,' laughed Adam.

Colin quickly retrieved the ball back and set about attacking again.

'I forgot to say. I'm going to be looking at some houses. Well, flats, but still… Be cool to have a place of my own.'

'That's massive, man. Think of the house parties! Is Simon showing you around?'

'Yeah, be a good chance to spend a bit more time with him. Reckon he might let a bit more slip if he feels he is in control of the situation. Get him on his own patch, so to speak.'

'Great idea.'

'So,' Colin said. 'I'm joining a rowing team and spending time house shopping with the captain of my soon-to-be rivals. I feel like I'm doing the heavy lifting here. What's your next move?'

'I'm going to go and visit Elena Henderson at home, see if I can learn a little bit more about Matthew. We still don't know if something fishy actually went on—it could've been an accident like the police thought. It could also be suicide.'

'I'd not thought about that.'

'Nor me, until yesterday. I want to see if there's any medication in the bathroom cabinet or something like that, something that might give us a hint.'

Plans set, attention turned in earnest to the pixelized players on the screen.

10

INITIATION

COLIN LEFT WORK the next day with a knot in his stomach.

As he walked to his car, he thought about his plans for the evening. The Meadowfield team were due to practice and they were expecting him. He'd managed to get in touch with a man called Jim who had intimated that they could do with all the help they could get.

Colin drove home, his thoughts on what he would say, how he would act and what persona he would put out to the Meadowfield team.

He was worried that they would know who he is. The towns were small and not that far away from each other—it was a part of the world where everybody seemed to know someone who knew someone who knew you.

There were no secrets.

Well, some. But not many.

He arrived home, ate dinner quickly and then went upstairs. For some reason, deciding what to wear was weighing heavy on his mind. He didn't want to look too keen, walking in dressed head to toe in sports gear. But he also didn't want to risk creating a bad first impression that would dissuade people from talking to him.

In the end, he chose tracksuit bottoms and a fitted T-shirt that showed off his toned arms. It was a warm night and if he could show that he may be an asset to the team, that might stand him in good stead.

He made his way back downstairs, fended off questions from his parents about where he was going and what he'd be doing, before finally escaping to the sanctuary of his car.

The journey to Meadowfield took about twenty minutes and he spent it all on the phone to Adam. They discussed what he might uncover and how he was potentially walking into a nest of vipers. He cut the call when he saw the sign for the neighbouring town's rowing shed and indicated, before turning down the narrow track.

No going back now, he thought.

HE PARKED HIS car alongside the others. Most had some sort of SUV or jeep and his hybrid Hyundai stuck out like a sore thumb. For a moment, he sat in the driver's seat, his stomach roiling and his head telling him to leave.

Leave now. Don't look back.

His almost jumped through the sunroof at the sound of someone knocking on his window. He glanced over to find an amused face peering through the glass. Colin held up a finger and made a show of collecting his bottle from the passenger footwell before climbing out of the car.

'Colin?' the man asked.

'That's me. And you're Jim?'

'Indeed. Thanks for the call today. It's great to have another set of hands on board. We're in desperate need of them.'

The two men shook hands and sized each other up.

Jim had a bushy moustache and greying eyebrows to match. His weather-beaten skin and lithe frame suggested that he had spent most of his working life outdoors and his friendly demeanour hinted that he was all the happier for it.

The callouses on his fingers scratched against Colin's smooth hands and he immediately felt self-conscious, as if his worth to the team could be judged by said softness.

'Shall we get started?' Colin asked, hoping to show how keen he was, despite his baby-smooth hands.

'Let's,' nodded Jim.

They walked towards the boat shed. It was smaller than the one in Stonebridge. The building was red brick and single storey.

One garage-style door was open, giving the rest of the team access to the equipment stored inside.

Colin and Jim entered the room and were greeted with stony silence. The Meadowfield team sat on folding chairs, angled towards the door.

Towards him.

'Alright, pal?' one of the men said, while the rest held their silence. 'Where did you say you were from?'

Colin just had time to note the man's trimmed goatee and camouflaged shorts before the door slammed closed behind him, shrouding the room in darkness.

'I… umm,' Colin stammered, fear tightening a knot in his stomach.

What had he walked into?

Did they know that he was here with an ulterior motive? Had they somehow found out that he was from their rival town?

Suddenly, a light flashed into life above his head and the laughter commenced.

'Sorry, mate,' the man who had greeted him said, leaping up from his chair. 'We're just messing with you. My name is Ricky. Welcome to the team.'

'You prick,' Colin managed, as the two men shook hands to a chorus of laughter. He could hear the blood rushing in his ears as the adrenaline coursed through his body.

Ricky introduced him to the rest of the team and he was afforded a warm welcome from everyone.

Well, almost everyone.

Unlike the rest of the team who had left their chairs to introduce themselves, the man in the corner of the room had remained seated. His long, ginger hair was gathered on his shoulders and small, crab-like eyes seemed to penetrate Colin, as if searching for a secret.

Colin looked back at him, keen to appear aloof to the hostility. He even managed a weak smile, which wasn't returned. Instead, the man produced an E-cigarette from his pocket and took a long puff, exhaling a cloud of smoke that seemed to envelope him.

'Right,' shouted Jim. 'Let's get the boat in the water and do some bloody work. We've only got a week or so left until the race.'

The room became a hive of activity as the men moved with a practiced fluidity to where they were needed. Ricky's iron grip clamped down on Colin's shoulders and he led him outside while the rest of the team got ready.

'Everyone here is alright. Paddy in the corner there just got out of jail a few months ago and is a bit wary of new faces. He really is a solid geezer when you get to know him.'

Prison!

'What was he in prison for?' Colin asked.

'Never you mind,' came the reply. 'Just pull your weight, give your all and he will soon come round to you. Alright, sunshine?'

The rest of the team emerged from the boatshed; the long canoe hoisted above their heads. They walked to the riverbank and delicately placed the vessel on the water.

After a few minutes, the canoe was filled and Colin genuinely felt terrified. He was about to enter open water, trapped in a claustrophobic boat, with a man (or men) who could possibly be behind the murder of the rival team's captain, as well as an ex-con.

'Ready!' shouted Jim, and he used his oar to push the boat away from the safety of dry land.

Here goes nothing, thought Colin.

COLIN SAT IN the bar after, his muscles tired and his body cold, but his spirit high.

He couldn't remember the last time he'd had such fun.

Already a keen proponent of exercise, he had excelled in pushing his body to the limit. It had taken him a while to find his rhythm, but once he'd discovered it, he had revelled in helping push the small craft through the choppy water.

There was something primal about it.

The congratulatory pats on the back from the rest of the team had been a welcome surprise, as had the invitation to join them in the bar for a quick pint after the equipment had been safely stowed away.

He took a sip of his beer and listened to tales that had probably been told a hundred times before, but had been pulled out once more for the newcomer.

He laughed along at all the right parts and began to feel part of the team.

And that's when he noticed Paddy, sitting in the corner of the room with a sullen look on his face. He was looking out of the window at the rapidly deteriorating light.

Colin's instinct was to walk over and strike up conversation, though Ricky seemed to be able to telegraph his feelings.

'I wouldn't, mate,' he whispered. 'Besides, I've got something else in mind for you.'

He winked at a few of the others lads, who finished the dregs of their pints and got to their feet.

'Come with us. It's time for your initiation.'

COLIN HAD WATCHED footage of many a footballer croon a stone cold classic a cappella, murdering it in the process, as part of their initiation after a big money transfer.

That's what he thought the Meadowfield team had in mind for him. He'd even picked Sweet Caroline as his tune, hoping that the crowd participation parts would see him through.

Thoughts of Neil Diamond were quickly pushed from his mind as he was bundled into the back of a car which was driven off at high speed up the narrow track. The car raced on the familiar coast road between Meadowfield and Stonebridge, and Colin was surprised at how little time it had taken to make it back to his hometown.

He was even more surprised when they entered the car park behind the town centre. The barriers were up to signify that no payment was necessary.

And why would it be? It was nearly ten o'clock and all the shops were shut.

'Right,' Ricky said, tossing him a bag inside which something clinked together noisily. 'Your mission, should you choose to accept it, is to walk to the offices of one Mr Holland and graffiti his shutters.'

Colin glanced inside the bag and felt his mouth grow dry. Two paint canisters, red and blue, appeared to look back at him accusatorily.

'Why?' he spluttered.

'Why?' Ricky laughed. 'To show that you've got balls. To show that you hate these scumbags as much as we do. To give two fingers to the people of this crappy town.'

The two other men in the car laughed loudly.

'What should I write?'

A series of choice phrases were hurled his way.

'Any of those,' Ricky said. 'Or, if you're feeling creative, you can make something up. We won't be offended that you disregarded our suggestions.'

With a small nod of the head, Colin got out of the car. He walked towards the town centre, weighing up what he had been asked to do. If he was caught, which was unlikely given the time of day and how dark it was, it would have serious repercussions—one more serious than the rest.

He could lose his job.

And he didn't want that.

On the flip side, he was committed to holding up his end of the bargain. Adam had promised Elena Henderson that they would look into Matthew's death and for better or worse, this would help.

Surely, once he'd done this, the Meadowfield team couldn't question his commitment. He could start asking his questions in earnest.

Maybe even ex-prisoner Paddy would be impressed and let his guard down.

He sighed and skulked around the corner towards the estate agent's office. Aware that there were no CCTV cameras down this end of town that could capture what he was about to do, he ran to the metal shutters, pulled out a paint canister and sprayed a message as quickly as he could.

Once finished and without even bothering to check his handiwork, he threw the cans back into the bag and legged it down the street towards the car park. The muscles in his legs were burning when he rounded the last corner and he stared across the swathe of concrete in disbelief.

The car park was empty.

'Dicks,' said Colin to the desolation, before taking off at pace again, keen to put distance between himself and the vandalism he'd just been forced into.

When he'd gone far enough, he pulled his phone from his pocket and navigated to Adam's name, though his finger hovered over the number without pressing it. He wasn't sure he was ready to explain what had happened tonight; hadn't had time to process it himself yet, and Adam would have a million questions.

Instead, he dialled a taxi, shame at what he'd done causing his cheeks to burn.

11

NOTHING LIKE NARNIA

'THEY WANTED YOU to write *the C word* with spray paint?'

Adam couldn't believe what he was hearing. He increased the volume of his speakers and strained his ears to try and hear what Colin was saying over the whine of his car's engine.

'That, amongst other things.'

'And what *did* you write?'

'Meadowfield rules. With a Z. I thought that way the police, if they are called, wouldn't suspect a Stonebridge resident as the person behind it, and secondly, it might start some sort of civil war.'

'Where people get sloppy with their secrets… I like it. It was a risky thing you did, though, but a potential gamechanger. Well done, mate. The Meadowfield team will probably let their guard down now that they think they can trust you. Do you think any of them could be capable of drowning a man?'

'Maybe,' said Colin, his voice echoing around the car. 'There's another practice tonight so I'll see what I can dig up. From what I can tell, Jim is the point of contact but Ricky is in charge. He's the one all the lads look up to. He seems like a bit of a thug.'

'You're telling me. I can't believe what they made you do.'

'It's done. Let's not go on about it. There's this lad called Paddy, too—fresh out of prison and with some of the looks he was giving me; I'd suggest it won't be his last stretch either.'

'Prison? Jesus. We're in deep here, aren't we?' replied Adam. 'I'm just pulling up at Elena's house now so I'll have to go, but I'll chat to you tomorrow after tonight's practice for a proper catch up.'

He hung up and drove slowly down the street, scanning the numbers for the correct house. He hadn't wanted to give Elena prior warning of his visit, so that he would be able to question her without having given her time to rehearse her answers. But, he'd hit a snag.

He didn't know where she lived.

His mother had come up trumps, though, sieving through a pile of Stonebridge Gazettes and finding the obituary notice, which listed the address as part of the funeral arrangements.

It was odd, he thought, how much people of a certain age bloody loved the obituary section of a newspaper. His granny used to say that it was the only reason she bothered with the local paper at all.

His mum used to despair at her, and now she was exactly the same!

When he reached number 75, he was surprised to find two cars filling the narrow driveway. One, a sleek black Audi and the other a pink Mini.

He didn't want to block them in, so drove further up the street until he found a bit of unoccupied kerb. He performed a rather graceless parallel park and got out, sighing at how far away he was from the kerb, but not caring enough to do anything about it.

When he reached the Henderson household, he climbed the steps and rang the doorbell. He listened for the chime but couldn't hear it, wondering whether it was out of use, or just very quiet.

He waited a few minutes before knocking on the door, not wanting to appear too pushy if the doorbell had indeed sounded.

There was still no answer. He cast a stealthy glance over his shoulder and tried the handle, though, it didn't budge.

He considered leaving it. She was either out or busy. As he turned to leave, another thought struck him.

If someone *had* killed Matthew, could his recently widowed wife also be in the firing line? Perhaps this had nothing to do with rowing and everything to do with the Hendersons.

That's probably why she hired me in the first place, Adam thought. *To make sure she wasn't about to be chopped up into mincemeat by some maniac.*

He could feel his blood fizz. He simply couldn't walk away, could he?

He ran through his options. He could call the police, but if they came and it turned out she was simply at work, he could get done for wasting police time.

Calling Elena at her office was another option, though not a viable one as he was missing the key piece of information. He didn't know where she worked.

But surely if she was at work, she'd have gone in her car, which he assumed was the Mini.

Frustrated, he spent a few minutes looking around the outside of the house, before noticing that the back gate was off its latch. He walked into the back garden to find an overgrown lawn and flower beds being overrun by weeds.

A few months ago, he wouldn't have cared less, but the messy garden was getting to him. He decided that he'd offer to tidy it up for her, free of charge. It was the least he could do for the grieving widow.

He tried the back door handle, just in case, but it too was locked. Glancing around, something caught his eye. On the ground, just behind an empty plant pot, was a solitary smooth, grey stone.

He picked it up and turned it over in his hands, his suspicions confirmed. He'd seen one in a movie once, he couldn't remember which, but had thought it was an ingenious way of hiding a key.

He pressed the small button on the underside and slid the two halves of the "stone" apart, unearthing a key the same colour as the back door's handle.

Ordinarily, he wouldn't go barging into someone's house unannounced or uninvited, but he was worried that Elena was lying beyond the door, injured or worse.

He wiggled the key into the lock, turned it and pressed down on the handle. Surprised at how easy people made it to break into a house, he took a tentative step across the threshold into a modern kitchen.

'Mrs Henderson,' he called, though only silence greeted him.

He tried again, louder this time, though it ended in the same result.

He closed the door behind him and moved to the centre of the room, turning a full circle on his heels, hoping something would leap out at him.

Nothing did.

Unsure of what he was looking for, his search became more like an episode of "Through the Keyhole". He flung open drawers and had a look at the contents, before moving into the living room.

Everything in here was fairly standard – a couple of sofas, a television and a rather ornate fireplace.

Something bothered him, though. There was a lack of personal touches. Most couple's houses he'd been to had an annoying number of photos of themselves. It always struck him as rather vain.

This living room, on the other hand, had no photos whatsoever. It was as if Matthew had never lived here at all. Perhaps it was simply Elena's way of dealing with her grief, he thought.

Out of sight, out of mind, as they say.

He made his way cautiously up the stairs, keenly aware that the bloodied body of Elena Henderson may be waiting for him. The thought made him shiver.

Upon reaching the landing, he called out again.

He was surprised by the wobble in his voice, but unsurprised with the lack of reply.

Gathering his bravery, he shoved each door open with a swift push, breathing a sigh of relief as each room offered no bloodied body.

Safe in the knowledge that he wasn't contaminating a crime scene, he relaxed and thought about where to begin his search.

He remembered watching a black and white film about Joy Division a few years ago, and how Ian Curtis used to steal medication from medicine cabinets of people he would visit after school. Or something like that. It had been a few years since he'd seen it.

This memory led Adam to the bathroom. The room was painted a light green and was home to one of the most luxurious showers he'd ever seen. For a nanosecond, he considered trying it out, before remembering that this wasn't his house.

Instead, he turned to the mirrored cabinet above the sink and opened it. He was hoping that there might be a tube or two of tablets that might signal that Matthew was on some sort of antidepressant. Sad though the thought was, it could've pointed the finger at suicide, rather than murder.

Sadly, for Adam, all that was to be found was a couple of tubes of toothpaste and some hair grips.

He closed the door of the bathroom and made his way to the master bedroom. An immaculately made king-sized bed took pride of place, surrounded by heavy wooden furniture.

As he was about to check the contents of the bedside tables, a noise from outside disturbed him—a car's brakes squealing as it came to a stop.

Adam ducked down underneath the windowsill and listened intently as he heard two doors slam closed. He could hear the drone of continued conversation and the clicking of heels getting closer to the house.

Not daring to breath, he snuck a peak out of the window, before ducking back down again and swearing continuously under his breath.

Elena and another person—a man—were walking up the path towards the house.

Panic was rolling through his body in waves as he ran through his options.

One, he could come clean and simply reveal himself. Though, explaining what he was doing in a widow's bedroom—having let himself in—could be tough to pull off.

Two, he could attempt to get down the stairs and out of the back door by the time Elena had let herself in the front.

This plan was dashed immediately as he heard the door at the bottom of the stairs open with a click and the two voices became clearer.

Which led Adam to plan three. Not the greatest of the trio, but the only one now available to him.

Hide.

He looked around the room and settled on the huge oak wardrobe. He crept over to it and pulled the door open slowly, before crawling into it and easing the door closed again.

His heart was hammering as he listened to the footsteps on the stairs and the voices grow closer. As the bedroom door opened, he tried to become zen—to be as still and as silent as it was possible or a human being to be.

What he heard chilled him to the bone.

Elena, and whoever the man was, instantly started kissing. He couldn't see it, thanks to the solid manufacture of the wardrobe, but he could sure as hell *hear* it. That horrible squelch of saliva swapping.

Who was this mystery man? Adam thought, trying to zone out the sounds of clothes being removed. *And why was Elena kissing him (and more) mere weeks after her husband had disappeared?*

What followed was the most uncomfortable and shameful twenty minutes of Adam's life. He could do nothing to ignore the grunts, the utterances of pleasure or the bedsprings proving their worth and was close to rocking backwards and forwards when the whole thing had come to a climax. Literally.

'Do you want me to have a look at it now?' the man asked, once clothes had, presumably, been reapplied.

'No, I best get back to the office,' came Elena's reply. 'You can do it another day. It's a good excuse for you to come back again.'

They giggled as they left and Adam emerged from the wardrobe a short while later, once he was sure that the coast was clear, feeling very much like a perverted Peter Pevensie emerging from a Narnian peep show. He was pretty sure that at some stage in his life, he'd recount this moment to a professional psychiatrist.

But he couldn't dwell on that now. He had a theory that he wanted to present to Colin, though he may omit the details on how he came by said information.

12

A VIEW TO A KILL

COLIN PULLED UP in front of the house. It was a simple two up, two down in an alright part of town. No fuss, no muss.

He stepped out of his car and walked to the porch, keen to get out of the mizzle that was starting to fall.

He checked the handle, but the door was locked so he pulled his coat a little tighter and turned his eyes to the road. He didn't have to wait long.

A minute or so later, a black BMW pulled into the street and screeched to a halt beside Colin's parked car. Simon Holland emerged from the driver's side; hands held aloft.

'Sorry I'm late, mate. I've had a right morning of it. First, the police and then I got held up with the last client.'

The estate agent flashed an apologetic smile.

'But, I'm here now and ready to show you this wonderful property. Now, I know we spoke mainly about flats, but I reckon with your budget, we can push to a lovely little house like this beauty. What do you say?'

Colin voiced his approval as he moved out of the way, allowing Simon to unlock the door. Colin followed him into a deceptively spacious living room.

As he was given the grand tour, Colin's attention kept wandering. Simon had mentioned the police and Colin was in no doubt as to why he had been in contact with the authorities.

He found himself walking around the house with his hands in his pockets, worried that there was a small smudge of paint he hadn't managed to scrub off, feeling very much like a modern-day Lady Macbeth.

He nodded at all the right times and tried to sound enthusiastic when he was shown a feature of the house Simon thought particularly pleasing, though he knew he wasn't fooling anyone.

'Not the house for you?' Simon said, when they returned to the front door.

Colin mumbled something non-committal and Simon laughed.

'The beautiful thing about houses,' he answered, 'is that there are hundreds of the buggers. We'll find the right one for you yet, Cinderella.'

He laughed at his own joke, before saying goodbye.

'I hope it's nothing too serious with the police,' Colin called after him.

'Nothing to worry about,' he said. 'Just some graffiti at the office.'

'That's a shame. Do you know who did it?'

'Some of those pricks from Meadowfield. There's no CCTV so we don't know who, but the police think it's probably someone from the rowing team trying to intimidate us, but it isn't going to work.'

'Yeah,' Colin answered. 'Don't let it get to you. I hope you beat them.'

'So do I, mate. I could do with the money. Also, could you imagine losing to a town who have two words for a patch of grass in their name. We'd never live it down.'

They bade each other farewell and, after a while, Colin's heartbeat returned to a normal speed. It seemed he had gotten away with his Banksy moment and in doing so, will have earned the trust and respect of the Meadowfield team.

He checked his watch.

It was nearly time to exploit that trust.

COLIN WALKED INTO the rowing shed with an annoyed look on his face. He didn't want the Meadowfield lads to think that he was a pushover, and making him break the law before abandoning him was a pretty low thing to do.

Most of the team were already there. They cheered when he entered and Colin took this to mean that the news of his initiation had been passed around and that he had been "accepted".

'Sorry, mate,' Ricky said, throwing his arm around Colin's shoulders. 'I know it was a dick move, driving away, but it's what we've done with all the others.'

Colin grunted before sitting down and getting changed for the upcoming session.

'I'll but you a pint to say sorry afterwards, alright?' Ricky said, and Colin nodded.

'AM I FORGIVEN?' Ricky asked.

Colin couldn't help but laugh at the ridiculous face the other man was pulling.

'I suppose so,' he said.

Ricky punched him softly on the arm.

'That's my boy. So, what's your deal?'

Colin gave some scant details of his life, keeping them as general as possible.

'How did you get involved in the Meadowfield team?' Colin asked.

'My family have always been involved. Of course, my father did it for the fun of it, whereas I'm quite money orientated. All the lads are. Five thousand pounds split between nine is alright compensation for winning a race.'

'Would you do it if there was no money involved?'

'Probably,' said Ricky. 'Like I say, it's a tradition in my family and it's always a chance to get one over those Stonebridge dicks.'

He paused to take a sip of his drink before elaborating.

'The money is a nice bonus, and of course, it acts as extra motivation. Since the prize money became a thing, the Meadowfield team have taken it more seriously, but we've still never won it. But, this is our year.'

'You sound sure of that.'

'Well, we have you for starters,' he laughed, squeezing Colin's bicep. 'But, to be honest, I doubt the race will even be held.'

A devious grin spread across Ricky's face.

'But, how can you win a race if it hasn't been held?' Colin asked, confused.

'It's in the rules that, if for some reason one of the towns cannot field a full team, it's counted as a forfeit and the opposing team are awarded the money.'

He took another gulp of his pint.

'We have a plan. We thought that what happened with their captain might force them into forfeiting in advance, but they appointed a new captain—the estate agent—and just carried on.'

'You didn't think they would?'

'No, any decent group of friends would surely abandon in the race in his memory. But not Stonebridge. They appointed another captain the very next day, I heard.'

'The captain gets an extra share of the money too.'

Ricky looked suspiciously at Colin.

'I think I read about it in the newspaper last year,' Colin muttered.

They descended into quiet for a minute or two.

'You mentioned before about a plan to force them to forfeit,' Colin said.

'Yeah. It's nothing bad or anything. What we thought we could do is try and target some of the members of the other team; intimidate them a bit so that they don't turn up on the day. That way, we win the money without even stepping into the boat.'

Colin could feel the question rising in his throat and when it emerged, it came out as a whisper.

'Did you have anything to do with Matthew Henderson's death?'

Ricky looked furious at the accusation and, as he was about to answer, the door to the bar flew open and Paddy walked in.

'Everything alright, here?' he asked, registering Ricky's scarlet cheeks.

Ricky stood up and walked over to his friend. He nodded in Colin's direction.

'Col here reckons we had something to do with Matty's drowning.'

'Oh aye?' Paddy said, raising an eyebrow. 'And what if we did?'

13

SUSPECTS

ADAM AND COLIN got in the car park's lift and descended three floors, emerging at street level. They walked past the gym, the butchers and the recently refurbished hair salon that Adam's auntie worked in, though he couldn't spot her through the window.

They entered The Jet—a huge hanger of a place that combined a cinema, soft play centre, arcade and a couple of restaurants. It was a Stonebridge favourite and was, as ever, very busy.

Colin booked the tickets for the film while Adam queued for the snacks. It was a time saving ritual they had perfected over for years.

'The 7 o'clock is sold out,' Colin said, as he approached his friend. 'But I got us the last tickets for the half past showing.'

They walked to the arcade and gravitated towards the shooting game. Colin inserted a few coins into the machine and they picked up the guns, as a computerised voice told them about their upcoming mission.

As the assignment began, they picked up the discussion they'd been having in the car about what Colin had learned from the Meadowfield practice sessions.

'What happened after Paddy came in, then?' Adam asked.

'I nearly pooed my pants, that's what happened. Ricky jumped up, saying I'd accused them of Matthew's murder. Paddy said something vaguely threatening and when I started to stammer and apologise, they both laughed. They were bloody well having me on.'

'I thought you said Paddy was a moody so and so?'

'He was the first night, but apparently my act of illegal vandalism was all it took for him to warm to me.'

'So, do you think they *could* have had anything to do with it?'

Colin considered this. He'd been turning it over in his mind since last night and he still hadn't come to a suitable conclusion.

'I think if any of them were behind it, it would be either Ricky or Paddy. The rest, aside from the two hyenas who were in the car with Ricky and me, seem to do the practice and head home. Ricky also talked about a plan to intimidate the Stonebridge team, so that not all of them would turn up and they'd be forced to forfeit. That way Meadowfield would win the money without lifting an oar.'

'Devious swine,' Adam replied, pointing his gun at the corner of the screen and taking out a Yakuza at point-blank range. 'So, we can put Ricky and Paddy on our mental case board.'

'And Simon, I reckon,' said Colin.

'Because he's an estate agent? Did you not like the house he showed you?'

'Shut up. Not just because he's an estate agent, and no, actually, I didn't like the house he showed me. But there is something off about him—taking the captaincy from your dead mate and not caring that he died while they were on bad terms shows that he's not a nice guy.'

'A nice guy—no. But a killer?'

'Maybe. Most people kill for one of three reasons—money, revenge or sex. And in this case, he stands to take home at least a grand, instead of a few hundred quid if his team wins.'

The game ended as Adam's risky move backfired and his character ended up splayed on the floor in a pool of pixelated blood.

'Speaking of sex...' Adam said, as they walked towards the seating area.

'If this involves you, I don't want to hear it.'

Adam fake laughed and then relayed his unsavoury wardrobe experience. Colin listened, aghast, to his friend's story and when he'd finished, he burst out laughing.

'You do know how to get yourself into some almightily weird situations.'

Adam punched him on the arm.

'In all seriousness, though,' Colin continued. 'There's something fishy there. Having it away with some unknown man weeks after your husband has died is strange behaviour.'

'I think she could have something to do with it. Maybe she and whoever the man is planned it together.'

'But why would she engage our services to find out who killed her husband if it was her and an accomplice. That makes no sense, except if she wanted to throw everyone off the scent.'

'But the police had already put it down as an accident. Why dredge it up again?'

'Maybe whoever the man she was… you know… doing the dirty with is the killer and he is trying to get close to Elena so that he doesn't look like a suspect, but in doing so, is making himself look very much like a suspect.'

'So, what's next?' Colin asked.

'You keep going with the Meadowfield lot. Maybe now that Prisoner Paddy has come on side he'll open up. And I'll try and find out who Elena is sleeping with.'

Colin checked his watch and realised that the film was about to start. He ushered Adam towards the correct screen, showed the employee his ticket and walked through.

While Adam was faffing, looking for his ticket, Colin pulled out his phone to put it on silent. He saw that he had a missed call and a text message from a number he didn't recognise.

Call me. Paddy.

He showed it to Adam, who had eventually located his ticket in his jacket pocket. Adam told him to ring immediately.

Colin walked a little way down the wide hallway, past posters of soon to be released films, and pressed dial.

'Hello?' said Paddy, answering on the second ring.

'It's Colin, how are you man?'

'Good,' came the swift reply. 'Rick and me have been down watching those Stonebridge lads practice. They look good and don't seem to be in the mind of giving up. So, we've come up with a plan. Be ready to stay a bit later after practice tomorrow night. See you then, pal.'

He hung up and Colin walked back towards the screen. Adam had already gone in and Colin stumbled towards the seat in the darkness. He apologised as he nearly knocked over a young girl's popcorn and almost fell into the lap of a rather annoyed looking man.

Finally, he slipped into the empty seat beside his friend.

'Well?' Adam whispered.

'Paddy says they are planning to do something to the Stonebridge team tomorrow night. I don't know what.'

14

A TWINKLE IN THE TORCHLIGHT

ADAM REPEATED THE journey to Elena Henderson's house, parking in a similar spot further up the street. He checked his watch. He'd intentionally chosen to arrive at a different time of the day; seven o'clock seemed perfect. Late enough that she would definitely be home from work, but early enough not to seem inappropriate.

He walked up to the door and knocked twice.

He heard movement from behind the door and was shocked when Elena opened the door.

She was wearing a red, figure hugging dress that was definitely too formal for a night in, alone. A pair of towering heels lent credence to the idea. In her hand, she was holding an unopened bottle of wine.

However shocked Adam was, it appeared she was more so. Her wide smile formed a perfect circle as she let out a gasp at the sight of him.

Clearly, she had been expecting someone else, though she managed to pull it together.

'Adam, how are you?' she said, adopting a more sombre tone which was at odds with the outfit choice. 'Do you have any news?'

'I'm okay,' Adam answered. 'No news, yet. We're still asking around. I was wondering if you wouldn't mind me asking a few questions.'

She took an almost imperceptible glance at her gold wristwatch and bit her lower lip.

'It won't take long,' Adam urged, and she relented.

She let him in and closed the door. He walked into the living room that he had been in, without her knowledge, just yesterday. It felt odd.

'Make yourself comfortable and I'll get you a drink,' she said, indicating to the sofa. 'Wine?'

'Just some water, thanks. I'm driving.'

She entered the kitchen while Adam took a seat. In the few minutes she was gone, he could hear a flurry of beeps which presumably were coming from her phone. He imagined her texting whoever she was expecting to tell them to delay their coming over.

Finally, she emerged with a tumbler of water and a half-filled glass of red wine. She set the water on the coffee table and sunk into a chair, cradling the wine glass.

'I'm not keeping you from something, am I?' Adam said.

'No,' she replied. 'I'm expecting a friend over; a woman from work who has very kindly offered to check on me.'

The emphasis she put on the company being female was so obviously a front. Adam almost pitied her, though he appeared to accept her story without question.

'I just wanted to ask a few questions about Matthew. We spoke to a few of his teammates and they suggested that the Meadowfield team were trying to do things to intimidate our team. I was wondering did Matthew ever mention anything about this?'

'No. He didn't really talk about the rowing thing at all. He knew I wasn't really interested, so he kept it to himself.'

Suddenly, she gasped loudly.

'Actually, I do remember something he said. We had this big fight because he blamed me for losing some of his equipment. I said he must've forgotten to bring it home one night, but he was adamant that it wasn't at the sheds. Over the weeks, more of the lads complained about losing things and they were convinced that someone was stealing from them.'

'Did he ever say who?'

'He mentioned a guy called Theo. He kept going on about him because he was new this year and he didn't know if he could be trusted. In the end, nothing was ever proven.'

'So, there was inter-team fighting?'

She nodded.

'To be honest, I don't think any of them really liked each other.'

'Was Matthew ever scared of going to training?'

'No,' she said. 'He was this big, burly man who wasn't scared of anything. He often compared being captain to one of those Attenborough documentaries; as soon as the young guns sense a bit of weakness, they pounce. That's why he always sort of ruled with an iron fist. It made him unpopular but it kept the others in line.'

Matthew didn't sound like a nice man. In fact, to Adam's mind, he sounded like an egotistical dictator when in fact all he was, was a captain of an amateur team of rowers.

Adam wouldn't be surprised if he *had* been pushed in. He sounded insufferable.

'Can I use your toilet?' he asked.

She nodded and directed him, though of course he already knew exactly where it was.

He walked up the stairs and went to the bathroom, but didn't enter. Instead, he closed the door loudly from the outside before tiptoeing to Elena's bedroom. It was the only room he didn't get a proper look around yesterday (having been mainly confined to the wardrobe), and he was keen to rectify that.

He took out his phone and turned on the torch.

The room was a bit messier than it was the last time he'd been here, but nowhere near as disordered as his own. Black trousers and a cream blouse, what Adam imagined must be her work clothes, were strewn on the bed alongside the contents of her handbag.

He passed the torch over the room, feeling his face redden at the sight of the wardrobe.

He pushed the thoughts of squeaking bedsprings out of his head, knowing he only had a minute at most before Elena would start to wonder where he was.

Pretty sure that there was nothing suspicious to be found, he moved to turn the torch off, when he saw something on the bedside table sparkling in its beam.

He moved as quietly as he could across the room and lifted the small object.

A cuff link; perhaps one of Matthew's that she kept by the bed for sentimental reasons, but more likely, Adam thought, belonging to the man she had invited to her bed yesterday.

And then, he realised exactly who it belonged to. He'd bet his house that the capital H stood for Holland. He remembered Colin tell him about the kitsch cufflinks that the estate agent had worn when he'd visited the office for the first time.

Simon Holland—that's who she was banging!

The cheek of the man, thought Adam. First, he took the captaincy freshly vacated by the recently deceased Matthew and now he was shagging his widow.

Simon Holland was doing nothing to improve the public's perception of his particular profession.

As Adam made his way to the bathroom and flushed the chain, he considered if Simon could be behind Matthew's murder. It made sense. He was in a position to take the lion's share of the prize money and, more importantly from what he knew of the man, he was the alpha male of the team. That status was probably more important to him than the cash.

He made his way downstairs, considering whether or not to bring up Simon.

In the end, he decided to keep that information under his hat for now. He thanked Elena for her time and returned to his car.

Instead of driving home, he circled around and parked his car in a space that gave him a clear view of her house. He didn't have to wait long at all for her visitor.

Adam was unsurprised when a tall man with dark hair, rather than a female colleague, emerged from the black BMW. He walked up to the door and kissed a laughing Elena on the cheek, before they both disappeared inside.

Did the estate agent pose a danger to her? Or could Simon and Elena really have planned this together?

15

A FAULTY ARM

ADAM'S EYES WERE hurting from concentrating on the screen. This was the side of business that he wasn't too hot on. Sure, he could slave away happily in a garden for the day, but an hour of VAT receipts and tax notes were beyond his skill level.

He was doing something about that, though. On the side of the desk were the stack of books about business he had invested in. He'd ordered them online and had secreted them under his bed when not in the house.

He was sort of used to bumbling through life and buying the books had felt like a very adult step. A ridiculous one at that.

His head kept telling him that Adam Whyte wouldn't amount to anything, let alone a successful businessman. Businessmen wore expensive, tailored suits and carried briefcases filled with important documents. They didn't toil in gardens and get their hands dirty. Literally.

Truth be told, he'd rather show his mum his dubious internet history than the covers of *Starting a Business for Dummies* or *Understanding Accounting*. Showing those to anyone else would mean admitting that he was serious about something. And he wasn't ready for that pressure. Yet.

The doorbell rang and he heard his mum groan out of her chair to answer it. He supposed it was a parcel delivery or one of her friends, but when he heard Colin's rumbling voice floating through the floorboard, he panicked. He lifted his pile of books and stuffed them as quickly as he could into the wardrobe, wincing as they clattered noisily onto the wooden base.

Colin appeared a minute later, just as Adam slammed the wardrobe closed.

'You're very red faced,' Colin said, hovering by the door. 'Have I caught you in the middle of something?'

'Shut up,' Adam replied. 'I was just doing some work.'

'Is that what you're calling it now?'

For the next few minutes, Adam filled Colin in on what information he'd gleaned from his house visit last night. When he'd finished, Colin looked shocked.

'So, Simon Holland is seeing Elena Henderson?'

'It certainly looked that way from last night. And sounded that way from the day before that…'

'Jesus.' Colin rubbed his chin with that back of his hand. 'It seems a bit soon to be moving on, doesn't it?'

'That's if she hadn't moved on before Matthew did.'

'You think she was doing the dirty on him before he died?'

'I'm not sure, and I'm not the grief police, but if my husband had died, I don't think I'd be ready to start something new a few weeks later. I think there may have been a period of cross-contamination.'

'What a horrible turn of phrase,' Colin said, throwing a sock he'd found at Adam.

As Adam went to bat it away, the arm of his chair separated from the leather upholstery, causing him to fall forward and faceplant onto the floor.

Colin roared with laughter as his friend picked himself up, holding the snapped plastic arm of the chair in one hand.

'I've only just bloody bought this,' he moaned, checking the damage to the chair. 'I've got a full day out and about tomorrow, so I'm going to have to take it back today. You fancy coming along?'

'Sorry, man,' Colin said. 'I have to get back to work. Some of us have set hours!'

The friends said goodbye and Adam shouted good luck down the stairs. Whatever Paddy was planning for tonight, Colin would need all the luck he could get.

THE WOOD EMPORIUM'S car park was empty when Adam pulled into it. He turned the engine off and walked around to the boot. From it, he manoeuvred the bulky chair, getting his angles just right as the chair slipped out. He grabbed the snapped piece of plastic and wheeled the chair inside.

The bell above the door had barely started tinkling when Percy sidled out of the shadows, uttering a greeting that made Adam swear aloud.

'Sorry for the fright,' Percy wheezed. 'How can I help you?'

Adam showed him the damaged chair and produced the receipt when asked. Percy apologised profusely as he waddled down the centre of the shop towards the computer and till.

With his tongue between his teeth, he logged onto the computer and clicked the mouse a few times. He blew out a mouthful of air, disturbing the dust that had settled on the desktop.

'I'm ever so sorry about this.'

Percy clicked a few more buttons and then turned the screen around so that Adam could see it. On it was a chair that looked almost the same as the one he had bought, but was several hundred pounds more expensive.

'They don't have the model you bought, and if they did, I wouldn't insult you by ordering the same one anyway, but they do have this one. Please allow me to exchange it for you, by way of apology.'

Adam tried to argue, and when that didn't work, he offered to pay at least some of the difference, but again his words fell on deaf ears.

'I think Jacob is up at the warehouse doing a stock check today, so I'll give him a ring and sort out delivery. He doesn't let me go up there anymore, on account of my back and I'm secretly glad. Stock checking is the most boring of all the jobs.'

He offered a small smile, before continuing.

'Anyway, I'm babbling. We'll be in touch. And once again, I'm very sorry for the inconvenience caused.'

Adam assured him one more time that it'd been no hassle, thanked him and walked out of the shop with a Wood Emporium Regatta weekend newsletter under his arm and a different opinion of the old man.

Percy Wood was alright, even if he had scared the bejeezus out of him at the start.

16

NEFARIOUS DEEDS

'YOU SEEM JUMPY, Colin.'

The words, spoken by Paddy, pulled Colin from his trance-like state in the back seat. He looked into the face of the ex-prisoner and forced a smile.

'Nah, man. I'm just a bit pissed that you won't tell me what we're about to do.'

'All in good time,' Paddy replied, while casting a glance at Ricky in the driver's seat.

Colin turned his attention back to the passing scenery. He rested his head against the cool glass and tried to slow his pulse by adopting some of the mindfulness techniques he'd been teaching the old folks at work.

It didn't work.

Try as he might, he couldn't shake the feeling that Paddy and Ricky were about to include him in something that may be the wrong side of legal. Not for the first time, he wondered if he should just bin the whole charade off. Paddy and Ricky were nutters and, not for the first time, he dreaded to think how this could impact his job and his life.

Colin observed the two of them, in the front, whispering and giggling. He felt sick.

He watched as the outskirts of Stonebridge came into view and listened as Ricky lambasted his hometown. It struck Colin as incredibly childish to be slagging off the architecture of a supermarket, but Ricky seemed to be enjoying himself.

A few minutes later, it became clear where they were going. Ricky indicated down the narrow road towards the Stonebridge rowing team's practice shed and swung the car into the track at high speed.

Instead of driving all the way down, he pulled into a lay-by that was mostly obscured by the overhanging branches of the surrounding forest.

'Out,' he ordered, as he turned the engine off.

Paddy obliged, pushing the door open and running around to the boot. From it, he pulled a black box with a carry handle.

'What's that?' Colin asked as he climbed out of the back seat.

'It's our toy for the evening,' Paddy laughed.

Ricky and Paddy set off walking down the track. The light was fading fast and the silence, punctuated only by the occasional cracking of a twig or a hoot from the forest, was unnerving.

When the building by the riverside came into sight, Ricky tugged the sleeve of Colin's jacket and pulled him into the edge of the treeline.

'Right, big man, here's the plan. We're going to go into their shed and cause some carnage. We've tried a few things now and nothing seems to be stopping them from competing, so it's time to up the ante.'

'Wasn't Matthew dying upping the ante?'

'For the last time,' Ricky snarled, 'we had nothing to do with that.'

Colin shrugged, trying to give off the impression that he didn't care one way or the other.

'Look man,' he said. 'All I want to do is have a share of the money, so let's do whatever crazy nonsense you have up your sleeves and get out of here.'

Colin wasn't sure if he sounded convincing or not, but Ricky and Paddy seemed to buy it. Before he knew it, they'd set off at pace towards the river. Colin followed them.

When he rounded the corner of the building, Ricky was already pushing a key into the padlock which held the metallic shutters tight to the ground. With a twist, they opened and Paddy began pushing them up into their holdings. The now uncovered door beneath was unlocked and they simply walked into the shed.

Inside, there wasn't much to see. Two canoes, stowed securely with the bottoms facing out, took up the back wall. A range of colourful kayaks filled another and a door on the bare wall led to the function room and bar area. A storage tub, filled with various sized oars, sat in the corner.

Paddy set the box he had retrieved from the boot of Ricky's car on the floor with a thump. A tinkle of metal sounded from within. The noise echoed off the concrete walls and floor.

'Shhh,' scolded Ricky.

'There's nobody within a mile of here,' Paddy shot back. 'Calm yourself.'

It was the first time Colin had seen a flare of anger from Paddy and it was an intimidating sight. The veins on his neck were popping and his teeth were bared like a wild animal.

'I'm calm,' said Ricky, holding his hands up in a placating manner.

Paddy, on his knees, undid the box's clasps and finally Colin set eyes on what was inside. He was, however, still clueless as to the actual intricacies of the plan.

Paddy lifted the drill out of the box and pressed the trigger. The end of the drill whirred into life. He lifted his eyebrows at Colin, as if expecting a compliment.

'What are you going to do with that?' Colin asked, confused.

In answer, Paddy pointed the drill at the canoes.

'We're going to drill a series of small holes into the bottom of the canoes, so that the Stonebridge team are unable to race. Therefore, they will have no choice but to forfeit.'

Ricky laughed. It sounded cold and cruel to Colin's ears.

'Imagine them at their next training session, when they realise there's water coming in. They'll not be able to point the finger at us because no one knows we have a key, and there'll be no sign of a break in. There won't be time to replace the canoes either, with the race being so close.'

Paddy was laughing now too. A high pitched, evil-sounding laugh.

Colin watched on as he carefully selected an appropriately sized drill bit and screwed it into place. He then got to his feet and approached the canoes.

Colin wracked his brains for some way to put a stop to this sabotage, but short of giving himself up, nothing came to mind.

Instead, he stood idly by as Paddy began drilling. The squeal of the metal drill bit penetrating the fibreglass was loud; almost disorientating. Colin clasped his temples and gritted his teeth, before nodding at the door to let Ricky know he was heading outside.

Once out in the fresh air, Colin took his phone out and was in the middle of composing a text to Adam when Ricky stepped outside too.

'Bloody noisy, isn't it?' he asked, as Colin quickly pocketed his phone.

'Horrible,' Colin answered.

'Look, I know all of this seems a bit extreme. But we need the money more than the Stonebridge team do. We know we can't beat them fairly, so this is the only way.'

'It doesn't sit well with me,' Colin said. 'I don't want anyone to get hurt.'

'They won't, mate. They'll put the canoe in the river and see that it's leaky immediately. It's an inconvenience at most.'

Colin deliberated on his next sentence, wondering how to word it best so as not to cause offence.

'Have you heard any whispers about what happened to Matthew?'

'This again? Look, all I know is from what the papers have said, that it was an accident. We had practice that night, so none of us could possibly have had anything to do with it.'

'Was Paddy at practice that night?'

Ricky took a few seconds.

'Come to think of it, no. He's only ever missed one and that was the night he wasn't there. But, I can assure you, he hadn't anything to do with it either. It was probably Matthew's missus that did it. Her, or he killed himself.'

'Why do you think that?'

'Ah, man. It's common knowledge that Matthew and Elena Henderson were heading for divorce. My brother worked with Matthew and he was proper down in the dumps for the last couple of months because of it. He was sure she was seeing someone behind his back.'

Well, hot dog, thought Colin.

As he was about to push Ricky for more information, Paddy poked his head out of the door.

'Oi, fishwives, we're done here.'

Ricky leapt into action, pulling the padlock from his coat pocket as Paddy rolled the shutters back down to the ground.

'Now, let's get out of here,' Paddy said, as they sprinted back to the car. As they clambered in and sped off, Paddy howled with adrenaline-fuelled laughter.

'Well, let's hope that does the trick.' Ricky said, entering the main road and decreasing his speed, so as not to stand out.

'Aye,' Paddy agreed. 'If not, we've only got one more thing up our sleeves and I'd prefer not to go there.'

17

A VIEWING AND A NO SHOW

A FEW DAYS had passed since Paddy's casual act of vandalism and Colin still wasn't sleeping well. Not well at all.

Every time he closed his eyes, the events in the boatshed kept playing on the back of his eyelids like some sort of drive-in cinema. He was worried sick that someone would find out he'd been involved, even under the guise of an undercover investigation. Which, he knew, would hold no weight with the police, and even less with his employers.

By the time the sun rose and it was time to get up, he had decided that night had been the final straw. He wouldn't be going back to the Meadowfield team. His undercover operation had come to an end with less than satisfactory results.

All he had learned was that Paddy and Ricky were fairly reprehensible characters and could well be behind Matthew's death, but were never going to admit it. He'd been coerced into taking part in their psychological games and been witness to physical sabotage of the other team's equipment. Both of them were closed books and were never going to admit to anything, so that was one dead end.

The other thing he had found out was that Matthew and Elena's relationship had been coming to a close before his passing. Perhaps that hinted at suicide. According to Ricky's brother's testimony, he'd been miserable for months. Maybe one night after practice, he'd finally had enough and thrown himself into the murky waters of the River Bann.

Or maybe Elena and Simon Holland were behind it. From what Adam had said, the two of them had seemed pretty cosy together. Maybe with Matthew out of the way, they were finally able to start a life they both wanted, but hadn't been able to have with Matthew alive.

Maybe Colin could lean on Simon a bit today during the viewing. Perhaps if he pretended to be super interested, the prospect of a sale may loosen the estate agent's tongue somewhat.

Speaking of which, if Colin didn't get a move on, there'd be no viewing!

THE HOUSE LOOKED promising from the outside. Even though it was a new build, it looked full of character—shutters on the side of the windows and a mint green door with a hefty lion head knocker.

It was in a nice part of town; affordable too, and he could imagine himself pulling up on the driveway after work and grabbing a beer from the fridge. Content, Colin sat on the steps outside with high hopes.

A few minutes later, a red Audi pulled up on the street outside and a suited man Colin recognised from the photos in the estate agents got out and walked towards him, hand extended.

'Jeffrey Morrow,' he said, wringing Colin's hand. 'Ever so sorry, but Simon couldn't make it today and he knew you were ever so keen on the property. We didn't want to let you down.'

Jeffrey led Colin into the house and showed him around. He enthusiastically pointed out features such as the south facing garden and the generously sized second bedroom, before inviting Colin to have a wander around on his own.

Having walked around it and got a feel for it, Colin fell in love with the house. The numbers worked for him and he was keen to do a deal, but first he wanted to know about Simon's absence. He walked back down the stairs towards the stand-in estate agent.

'I like it,' Colin said. 'I think I'd like to put an offer in.'

Jeffrey's face lit up. Colin's next words brought him back down to Earth.

'Since I've been dealing with Simon, I'd quite like to conclude my business with him though. Will he be in the office tomorrow?'

'Umm..' Jeffrey mumbled. Colin sensed that he was buying for time. He fixed him with a Paddington-style stare.

'The thing is… Simon hasn't been in the office for a couple of days and I can't get in touch with him. His phone is off. But,' he continued, regaining his professional mask, 'as partners, I can do exactly what he could. You're in safe hands.'

Jeffrey took a step towards the door, the look on his face suggesting that he couldn't wait another second to get back to the office and sign those papers.

'Exactly how long has Simon been missing?' Colin asked, as Jeffrey closed the door.

'He didn't come to work yesterday, nor today.'

'Have you phoned the police?'

Jeffrey actually chuckled.

'No, he's a big boy, who can look after himself. He's probably psyching himself up for the race. It's the day after tomorrow, you know?'

'Has he done this before?'

'No,' replied Jeffrey, absentmindedly. 'Though, it's his first year as captain. He has been snappier than usual in the office. I put in down to the added pressure. Anyway, shall we meet at the office and we can talk figures?'

Colin nodded and both men walked to their respective cars. As soon as he started the ignition, he dialled Adam's number.

JACK BAUER'S RINGTONE interrupted the music Adam was listening to. Yeah, the show hadn't been on TV for something like twelve years, but the *bloop bloop* of the tone always made him smile.

He pulled his headphones out, silenced the leaf blower and answered the phone.

'Good morrow, fair Colin,' he said, adopting a Ye Olde English accent.

His friend's reply was less friendly.

'Simon's gone missing. I'm going to ring Paddy and see if he knows anything, but he's unlikely to give anything away. Can you ring Elena and find out if he is at hers? There might be a perfectly reasonable explanation behind all of this, but with the race so close, something doesn't feel right.'

Adam confirmed he would, before hanging up. He found her number in his phone book and dialled.

'Hello,' she answered. She sounded angry.

'Hi, it's Adam Whyte.'

'I can see that on the phone display. What do you want?'

Adam was unperturbed. In his career with woman to date, he was used to them talking to him like something they'd stood on—if they'd even elected to speak to him in the first place.

'I was wondering if you'd spoken to Simon Holland recently?'

There was silence for a few seconds.

'Why would I be speaking to him?' she asked, finally, the venom of her last words replaced with a hint of confusion.

'Cards on the table, Elena. I saw him enter your house the other night after I'd left. I saw him kiss your cheek so I assume something is going on there.'

She attempted to interrupt, but he continued speaking.

'There's no judgement, okay? But I need you to answer me, have you spoken to him recently?'

There was more silence on the other end of the line, before a series of muffled sobs erupted in Adam's ear.

'No,' she said. 'I thought he was into me, but he's just like every other man. Once he got what he wanted, the communication stopped.'

'Can you remember the last time you did hear from him?' Adam said, attempting to interrupt her diatribe against men.

'Yesterday morning. We were arranging who was going to cook next and he was moaning about some damage to the canoes. We arranged to meet last night, but he never showed up and now my messages aren't delivering.'

'Elena, listen to me. We have reason to believe that something has happened to him. If you hear from him, please let me know.'

He hung up, phoned Colin back and relayed the conversation he'd just had with Elena.

'I don't think she's got anything to do with it. With Matthew or Simon. She was genuinely angry that he'd ghosted her.'

'Which leaves Paddy or Ricky,' replied Colin. 'Predictably, Paddy is denying any knowledge of Simon's disappearance. But, when we got back in the car the other night, he said he had one more idea up his sleeve in case the holes in the canoe didn't work.'

'And you think the contingency plan was kidnap?'

'With Paddy, who knows?'

18

A BREAKTHROUGH FROM AN UNLIKELY PLACE

ADAM LAY ON his bed, his mind whirring with thoughts he was finding hard to file in a helpful order.

They were at a sticking point. In his mind, Elena was innocent of any wrongdoing. Well, wrongdoing in the murder of her husband, anyway. And she probably had nothing to do with Simon's disappearance either.

Though the jury was out on whether her relationship with Simon Holland had started before or after Matthew's demise, that wasn't for Adam to concern himself with. Live and let live, as his mother said.

The troubling part was that Paddy and Ricky had had some sort of contingency plan in place, but wouldn't give any details as to what that plan was. It left Adam and Colin clueless, with a man's life potentially on the line.

Colin had spoken to Jeffrey Morrow again when he'd gone in to secure the house. Jeffrey hadn't appeared worried and was keen not to get the police involved, for fear of wasting their time, he'd said.

Adam and Colin had deliberated on the next step for a while earlier in the evening, but no real plan had emerged. Colin had suggested that they stake out the Meadowfield boatshed, just in case that's where Paddy and Ricky were keeping Simon. It had felt like a lot of effort for a maybe, considering both had work the next day.

In the end, they'd decided that what happened next was out of their hands. They'd been hired to investigate Matthew's death and, while there were still some suspicions, it was clear they weren't going to get any concrete answers tonight.

Adam had almost resigned himself to phoning Elena in the morning and telling her that they were going to stop investigating. And that, after another night of a no-show from Simon, it had probably become a police matter.

Sighing, he untangled his headphones and plugged them into the port on his phone. Recently, he'd been listening to podcasts before bed, as they seemed to relax him.

He found an episode he'd been half way through—*The Pitfalls of Business*—and pressed play. The American presenter's animated voice filled his ears as he fell back onto his pillow.

For a while he simply lay there, staring at the ceiling and listening as sleep crept up on him.

Suddenly, he shot up into a sitting position with a gasp. He unlocked his phone and rewound what he was listening to. The American had said something that had set off a series of thoughts in Adam's mind.

He listened again, to make sure that he had heard correctly.

"Debt can be the biggest driver towards not only your business failing, but towards you becoming someone who you don't like. It can make you do things you never thought you'd do, and treat people in a way that is not okay. It can turn you into a monster…"

Adam pulled the earphones out and went over to the desk. He pulled out the top drawer and found the plastic bag that contained the information he'd been given when he had bought the desk and chair from The Wood Emporium.

He laid his hand on what he needed and pulled it out.

The Wood Emporium Regatta newsletter.

He leafed through it and found the page he needed. Instead of an interview with then captain Matthew Henderson, there was a short celebration of his achievements, coupled with a mournful obituary.

Adam picked up his phone again and called Colin.

'I think I know where Simon is. And I think I know who killed Matthew Henderson.'

COLIN AND ADAM pulled up in a car park a short walk from the sprawling industrial estate. Adam pulled his coat on as they exited the car and they began walking towards the silhouetted warehouses.

'So, you think Jacob Wood is behind all this?' Colin asked.

'I do. When we went to buy my desk, he was slagging off his dad for sponsoring the race and putting up the prize money. He said they couldn't afford it and that his dad was putting sentimentality over the business. He also said that he was due to interview Matthew for the newsletter they put out. He was supposed to interview him on the night he died, but when Jacob got there, he claimed Matthew was nowhere to be seen.'

'You think Jacob did this to spite his dad?'

'No,' said Adam. 'I think he did it to try and have the race called off so that they wouldn't have to hand over five grand to the winning team. They've always got a sale on, so they must be in a pretty precarious financial position. I bet he thought that pushing Matthew into the river, if that's what he did, would put an end to this year's race.'

'But, it didn't,' Colin concluded. 'Instead, Stonebridge vowed to win it in his honour. So, Jacob had to go to plan B. You don't think he will have killed Simon?'

'I don't,' Adam confirmed. 'Too much heat for a small town. He'll have kidnapped him with the intention of freeing him as soon as the race was called off.'

'But, couldn't Simon just go to the police and tell them exactly who had him once he's been released?'

'I'm betting that Jacob somehow got to him without Simon knowing who it is. He was probably blindfolded and taken to the warehouse without knowing where he is.'

They were amongst the warehouses now. Adam could make out the one belonging to the Wood family, thanks to a small plaque to the side of the door that was being illuminated by the huge, neon sign of the cavernous Lyon's food service warehouse next door.

The front door of the Wood warehouse was shuttered, but a quick check around the perimeter of the building unearthed a back entrance.

Adam tried to jimmy the lock, but to no avail. It wouldn't budge.

Eventually, Colin took matters into his own hands and unleashed his size elevens. It only took a few kicks to free the door from its lock. Colin led the way.

IT WAS DARK inside the warehouse, the moon managing to provide only a small slice of light. Colin and Adam crept in quietly and listened.

At first, there was only silence.

And then, Adam heard it. The ragged breaths of someone close by.

He got out his phone, lit the torch and tiptoed towards where he thought the noises were coming from. The warehouse was full of wooden furniture and the layout reminded Adam of a maze. He wondered whether Jacob had laid it out like this on purpose.

The boys rounded a corner and there sat Simon Holland on a kitchen chair in a little alcove of the warehouse. He had a black bag over his head, though it was easy to identify him from the smart, pinstripe suit and chunky wristwatch.

'Who's there?' he uttered, the fear making his voice tremble.

'It's Colin McLaughlin.'

'The boy I'm trying to sell a house to?'

'Yeah,' Colin confirmed. 'Although, this is unrelated.'

He walked over to the estate agent and slipped the bag off his head. Simon's eyes narrowed at the beam of torchlight, which Adam quickly diverted away from him. Instead, he walked around the back of the chair and directed the light at the bindings, which Colin made short work of.

Free, Simon stood slowly on unsteady legs and massaged his raw wrists.

'Where am I?' he asked, his voice hoarse.

'Percy Wood's warehouse,' Colin answered. 'We think his son, Jacob, kidnapped you.'

'Bastard. Can I borrow your phone to call the police?'

Colin nodded and slipped his phone from his pocket. He unlocked it and handed it to Simon.

As he hit the third nine and hovered his thumb over the call button, a noise from outside stopped him. The industrial estate didn't get much passing traffic in the middle of the night, which meant that the roar of the engine must be approaching for a reason.

'No time for that,' Simon said, handing the phone back to Colin. 'But, I have an idea.'

They gathered around him as he revealed the details of his hastily put together plan, before getting into position.

19

CAN'T SEE THE WOOD FOR THE TREES

THE ENGINE NOISE got progressively louder until it sounded like the car might plough through the walls. Thankfully, it didn't. Instead, it swelled to a roar before stopping abruptly close to the front door, just like Simon thought it would.

Colin waited by one side of the door, crouched just underneath the light switch while Adam mirrored him on the other side. Simon stood in the aisle of the warehouse, the black bag back on his head. In the little light available, it was a terrifying sight.

Outside, the motorised hum of the shutters opening shattered the silence. Colin gave Adam a little nod to settle his nerves, which his friend returned.

How had they managed to get caught up in this? Adam thought.

The shutters clunked into their housing and keys jangled in the lock. With a click it opened and a hand appeared around the frame, fumbling for the light switch in the dark.

After a few attempts, he found it and with a flick, the room was illuminated.

Simon's plan immediately clicked into play. Jacob took one step into the warehouse and at the sight of the estate agent standing in the aisle with the bag over his head, let out a bloodcurdling shriek. At that, Colin rugby tackled Jacob from the side, taking him to the floor. While Colin secured his legs, Adam straddled his chest.

Simon pulled the bag from his head and walked over to the furniture seller. He bent over him and stared into his eyes.

'You prick,' he uttered, before tying his hands together and dragging him to a nearby chair.

WITH ASSURANCES THAT no one was going to hurt him (though Simon took some convincing), Jacob finally stopped whimpering. He pleaded to be untied, but was met with unsympathetic glares.

'Why did you kidnap me?' Simon asked, venom soaking every syllable.

'I thought that I could save the business that way. We're haemorrhaging money on rent and on good quality furniture that no one wants to buy. I thought that if the captain didn't turn up, the race would be called off and we'd have saved five thousand pounds.'

'Did you kill my friend?'

Jacob's chin sunk to his chest, his eyes fixed on the floor.

Simon took a threatening step towards him, but Colin intervened.

'Go outside and get some fresh air,' he said to Simon while handing him his mobile. 'And phone the police while you're at it.'

Simon looked like he wanted to dish out some stone-cold retribution, but Colin's level words seemed to sink in, as he turned and made his way through the open front door.

'Did you kill Matthew Henderson?'

Tears filled Jacob's eyes as he nodded once.

'I didn't mean to though. I was supposed to be interviewing him for the newsletter. Dad and I had just had a huge argument about our cash flow. He couldn't get it into his head that handing over five grand to the winner was a ludicrous thing to do in our situation.'

'So, you killed Matthew to stop the race?'

'Subconsciously, maybe,' Jacob admitted. 'I'd tried talking to Matthew a few weeks ago to try and get him to forego the prize money, but he'd said no. I thought he'd be sympathetic to our situation, but he couldn't have cared less. When I arrived at the boathouse to interview him, he goaded me straight away. He was so close to the water's edge and before I knew what I was doing, I'd hit him over the head. I immediately tried to grab him, but the currents were so strong that he was taken away before my very eyes.'

'And you didn't think about reporting it?' Colin asked, disgusted.

'I did. But then I thought better of it. I reckoned that with the team captain tragically dying, the race organisers might have made a compassionate call to cancel the race. When it didn't happen, I was livid. But I wasn't going to admit to murder. It looked like an accident and that's the way I thought it would stay.'

'Until you decided to kidnap the new captain?' Adam laughed. 'You realise that in a small town you were never going to get away with it?'

Jacob heaved a heavy sigh.

'Money makes you do crazy things. I was only ever trying to save the business and protect my family.'

'And in doing so, you've probably consigned your father's business to history. No one is going to want to buy furniture from a murderer.'

Jacob hung his head in shame as sirens filled the night sky.

20

THE STONEBRIDGE REGATTA

COLIN AND ADAM watched from the bridge as the canoes passed underneath. It was neck and neck with nothing to separate the two teams.

'You didn't fancy it in the end, then?' asked Adam.

'I think I might have suffered the same fate as poor Matthew had Paddy found out I was an undercover operative from Stonebridge!' laughed Colin.

In the distance, near the finish line of the race, a small stage had been set up next to a large screen, onto which live footage of the race was being projected. The boys followed the path by the river towards the finish line, eager to find out who'd won.

TEN MINUTES LATER, the judges were still deliberating over a photo finish. It was the closest race in the history of the regatta, and both teams were sat by the riverbank in two separate camps.

A microphone squeaked, causing many in the crowd to jump in surprise. Their attention was diverted to the stage, where the mayor of Stonebridge stood, with Percy Wood beside him.

'Ladies and gentleman, boys and girls,' started the mayor, doing his best impression of a circus ringmaster. 'The results are in. The winner of this year's Stonebridge Regatta is…'

He stopped, surveying the crowd with a wide smile, milking the moment.

'It's not bloody X factor, pal!' someone shouted near the front, causing a gale of laughter.

'Keep your hair on,' retorted the mayor with a smile. 'The winner is Meadowfield!'

A mixture of cheers and jeers filled the air as the Meadowfield team jumped to their feet and began a chorus of "Championes!"

The despondent Stonebridge team, led by Simon, got to their feet and formed a guard of honour for the winners to walk through on their way to the stage.

Percy Wood took to the microphone as the winning team received their medals.

'Congratulations to the Meadowfield team on a fine win. Before the trophy is presented, I would like to offer a sincere apology on behalf of the Wood family. My son's actions were not those of an honest man. What he did will haunt me to my dying day, and I only hope you do not associate his heinous actions with the family name.'

He gave a small sniff as the crowd applauded him.

'The business will be closing for good next week and I am delighted to hand over a cheque for five thousand to each team.'

The Stonebridge team's necks collectively whipped around at breakneck speed to look at the stage, to be sure that what they heard was correct.

And it was.

Percy was holding two oversized cheques, totalling ten thousand pounds.

As the celebrations began in earnest, Colin and Adam began walking home.

'That's two murders we've solved now,' Adam said. 'We're making a name for ourselves. I might give up the gardening and go full time.'

'Might be slow business—surely that's Stonebridge's excitement quota reached for a few more years.'

Adam nodded, and the two of them walked in silence.

'When do you get your new house?' Adam asked, after a while.

'Not sure,' Colin replied. 'Should be pretty quickly though. There's no chain to hold it up so it should be good to go in a few weeks' time.'

'I might be joining you.'

'In my house?' Colin asked.

'No, dickhead. In buying my own. Simon was so thankful to us for rescuing him that he told me he could get me a good deal on a flat in the centre of town.'

'Look at us moving up in the world,' Colin laughed. 'Our mothers will be so proud!'

ABOUT THE AUTHOR

Originally hailing from the north coast of Northern Ireland and now residing in South Manchester, Chris McDonald has always been a reader. At primary school, The Hardy Boys inspired his love of adventure, before his reading world was opened up by Chuck Palahniuk and the gritty world of crime. He's a fan of 5-a-side football, has an eclectic taste in music ranging from Damien Rice to Slayer and loves dogs.

Lightning Source UK Ltd.
Milton Keynes UK
UKHW012141180621
385769UK00002B/80